PEAS AND HAMBONE VERSUS FLESH-EATING ZOMBIE GORILLAS

by

TODD NICHOLS

ISBN: 0615871003
ISBN 13: 9780615871004
Library of Congress Control Number: 2013915583
CreateSpace Independent Publishing Platform
North Charleston, South Carolina

Chapter One

My name is Peter.

But you can call me Peas. That's P-E-A-S. Like the vegetable. Not like the other kind, the one with the two *e*'s that's not a vegetable at all. Has nothing to do with little green spheres or giant green...well, giants. Ho—ho—ho.

No.

The one with the two *e*'s has to do with a certain bodily function we all do, but it's not like I want to spell it out for you.

Here's a clue: it has to do with yellow streams and "Don't eat the yellow snow!"

Which is gross, but I've seen a kid do it.

I'm thinking about the time Joey Zabroski convinced Marcus Winkleman that the yellow snow tasted like a lemon snow cone—so he ate it. Gobbled it all down and even said he like the tangy taste. If you can believe it.

Marcus isn't that bright. He says it's because his older sister dropped him on his head when he was a baby. But I don't think that's the reason. I think it's because of all the yellow snow he's eaten in his life. It can't be good for brain functioning.

I mean, here's another example. Just the other day, Joey had Marcus convinced that another bodily function left behind by a dog on the playground was a Tootsie Roll. And if I hadn't stopped him, he would have gobbled it all down, too. I just know it.

I don't even want to think about what he would have said after doing that. Tastes like...No! I don't want to think about it. I'm blotting it out from my memory. Even as I'm telling you this.

So back to what I'm telling you.

Peas is my nickname. And before you start in on how stupid that nickname is, let me just say that I agree with you. It's a stupid nickname. I have no idea why my dad started calling me that. I just know that ever since I can remember, that's what he's called me.

So why am I telling you this?

Why am I opening myself up to embarrassment and potential ridicule by letting millions of people know my stupid nickname?

I'm telling you this so you can see for yourself what kind of kid I am. I want you to see that I'm not the kind of kid who's going to you-know-what on your leg and say it's raining. (Think the one with two *e*'s.)

No.

I'm honest. Straight out, I'm going to tell you the truth, no matter the cost to me or my reputation.

This is important. It's important because of what I'm going to tell you next.

I have a dog. His name is Hambone.

I know. Not earth-shattering news. But here's the earth-shattering part: the thing about Hambone is that he's not only a dog—he's also a kid. Just like me. Whenever he wants, he can walk on two legs and talk and do everything any kid can do.

Impossible, you say? I thought so at first too. (I mean, it's not like I've been eating yellow snow all my life.)

But it is possible. But only when Hambone is with me.

He doesn't do it when other people are around.

I didn't know this at first. So I told my family that Hambone is not a dog but a kid even though he doesn't look like a kid, he looks like a dog.

Of course, that didn't go over real well.

My mom and dad both laughed and said I was crazy.

My older brother went further and said I wasn't just crazy, I was loco, nuts, cuckoo for Cocoa Puffs, out of what little mind I have, etc. He said I should be wrapped tight in a straightjacket and taken to the loony bin. Which sounds like a fun place. Maybe that's where they keep all the Looney Tunes characters like Bugs Bunny and Elmer Fudd. That would be a pretty cool place to go. So long, Sammy, see you in Miami. Just kidding.

But what was I saying?

Oh, yeah. My family thinks I'm crazy.

I told Hambone this. He laughed. He said that I should let them think that. He said that whenever anybody sees us together, he'll make sure to go back to being a dog doing dog stuff. So nobody will ever know the truth. It will be our little secret, he said.

Well, now it's ours and yours.

But you have to swear not to tell anybody else.

If you do that, we're cool.

Besides, if you tell people, they're going to think you're crazy.

And you don't want that.

You might wind up in the loony bin.

So we're cool?

Good.

Because what I really want to start telling you about is the time me and Hambone had to stop Evil Doctor Crazy Gorilla from taking over the world. His plan was to create an army of zombie gorillas dead set on eating the flesh of every human on the face of the planet until there weren't any humans left. Only zombie gorillas.

And his plan would have worked, too, if it weren't for me and Hambone.

We saved the human race.

But I'm getting ahead of myself.

Before we saved the human race, we went to the zoo.

And that's where it all started.

CHAPTER TWO

I'm standing in front of Hambone, trying to block any of the zoo workers from seeing what he's doing.

Which is digging a hole underneath the fence that surrounds the zoo.

I can hear Hambone cursing to himself as he digs.

Somebody filled in the hole he made yesterday. So now he has to dig another one.

"If I find out who did this, they're gonna be sorry," he says. "Maybe leave a nice little calling card on the roof of their car, if you know what I'm saying."

"Maybe they're on to us," I say.

Hambone sniffs. "Doubt it," he says. "But if you think so, you'd better keep a good lookout."

I keep a good lookout.

Out of the corner of my eye, I see something moving. A car is pulling into the zoo's parking lot.

"Pssst," I say over my shoulder. "Ixnay on the diggingay."

Hambone doesn't stop digging.

The car comes closer to where we are. It stops.

I just know that the people in the car are looking right at us, wondering what we're doing. Maybe they know what we're doing and are calling the cops.

I try not to make eye contact. If I don't make eye contact, I can pretend the car really isn't there.

It's a little trick I developed. If you don't want to believe something that really is there is there, just don't look at it. And it will cease to exist. Believe me, it works every time.

It works again.

When I look over—because I have to look; it's absolutely killing me not to look—the car is gone. I see it heading out of the parking lot and onto the road.

Phew!

Just somebody using the parking lot to turn around. Probably lost or wanting to go in a different direction.

But still. That was close.

I start to get nervous. What if another car pulls into the parking lot? Not somebody who's lost, but somebody who's coming to the zoo. The zoo doesn't open for another hour, but what's to stop some family from getting here a little early? Trying to be first in line?

That's what my dad does. Any place he goes, he has to be the first one there. Right when the place opens. It's not fun for me. Because I have to sit in the car with him trying to think of something to do to kill the time.

I just know the world is filled with more first-in-line nuts like my dad. And they'll show up any second.

I don't like this. We were lucky nobody saw us yesterday.

I turn to face Hambone.

"Why don't we just wait for the zoo to open like everybody else?" I say.

"Are you kidding me?" says Hambone, not looking back. "I'm not paying seven dollars to look at a bunch of dumb animals. If I wanted to do that, I'd just look in the mirror. Save the seven bucks."

He stops digging and thinks about what he just said. "That didn't come out right. But you know what I mean. Pay like everybody else? Where's the fun in that?"

I look down at the hole I'm going to have to crawl through.

"This is fun?" I say.

"The fun is in doing something dangerous—something that will get us into trouble if we get caught," says Hambone. "That's the juice. The jazz. What makes us alive. And what separates us from those dummies in their cages." He nods his head in the direction of the zoo's entrance.

I guess now is as good a time as any to tell you that Hambone likes to get into trouble. He can be a very bad dog. And since I'm always with him—he's my best friend, you know—I end up right in the middle of whatever trouble he's getting into.

Like now.

Hambone stops digging.

"There," he says, standing up. "That should be good enough. See if you can fit through."

I get down on my stomach and begin to army-crawl under the fence. I fit my head through just fine, but then the collar of my shirt gets snagged on a piece of wire jutting out.

I carefully rock back and forth to try and get unsnagged.

It doesn't work. All it does it get me more snagged. And now I can feel the piece of wire against my skin. It feels like the knifelike fingernail of Freddy Krueger, that *Nightmare on Elm Street* guy.

My older brother loves watching those movies. I don't. But he sits on me and forces me to watch them with him even though he knows they scare the you-know-what out of me. (Think the one with two *e*'s.)

I stay perfectly still.

If I make a sudden move, Freddy Krueger's fingernail...um, I mean, the piece of wire will slice into my flesh. Maybe hit an artery.

I can just picture it. Like in those *Nightmare* horror movies. Blood starts spurting out like a volcano erupting. But I can't stop it. I can't reach my finger back and plug up the artery. I'm snagged good. All I can do is wait helplessly as the gushing blood fills up the hole I'm lying in, getting higher and higher until I drown in a pool of slimy, red dirt.

Oh, the horror.

Of course, that's not going to actually happen. But what if it did? Hambone doesn't have any fingers to plug up my artery. And if he runs for help, nobody will believe him. He's not Lassie, you know.

"I could use a little help here," I say.

Hambone puts his foot on my butt.

"What are you doing?" I say. "Are you crazy? Don't you see that wire I'm caught on? Do you want it to slice me open?"

"If you die, you die," says Hambone.

I think he's joking.

I hope he's joking.

With his foot still on my butt, Hambone shoves me as hard as he can. I'm propelled through the hole and onto the path that snakes all through the zoo. In the process, the wire tears a hole in my shirt but doesn't do any damage to my flesh. I'm lucky.

"What were you thinking?" I say.

"Don't be such a baby," says Hambone, crawling under the fence and joining me on the path. "There's not a scratch on you."

"But there could have been."

"But there's not. So let's go."

We walk past the signpost pointing to the reptiles.

We walk past the signpost pointing to the Mexican gray wolf.

We walk past the signpost pointing to the peacock place.

This zoo has everything.

If I didn't know where we were going, I'd be lost.

But I know where we're going.

We're going to the Gorilla Kingdom. It wasn't open yesterday for some reason, so Hambone said it would be our first stop today.

I follow Hambone down this path that has all these trees on either side so it looks like we're walking through a forest. Once we get through the forest, the path opens up into this clearing. That's where all the gorillas do their gorilla stuff.

I hate going to the Gorilla Kingdom. I hate it because they smell.

According to one of the signs the zoo put up, they want you to immerse yourself in the sights and sounds and smells of the gorillas. But the more I immerse myself, the more I want to take a shower after—the gorillas have major stink issues. You'd think somebody would hose them down every once in a while.

Maybe I hate the smell because it reminds me of how my brother likes to immerse my face in his armpits. Especially if he's just exercised for like ten hours.

Hambone isn't a big fan of the Gorilla Kingdom either. But for a different reason.

He doesn't hate the gorilla smell, he just hates the gorillas. In fact, he says he has

a special kind of hate for gorillas. (I think it stems from some childhood trauma involving the movie *King Kong*.)

So why is he going to the Gorilla Kingdom?

Revenge.

Last summer one of the gorillas picked up some dirt and threw it at Hambone. Not on purpose. At least, I thought it was all very innocent like. But Hambone didn't see it that way. He took it personally. As if the gorilla had done it on purpose because he knew how much Hambone hates gorillas. And ever since that day, he swore he'd get even.

"Do you know what I'm going to do to that gorilla when I see him again?" says Hambone, stopping at the moat at the edge of the clearing.

(I think it's funny that it's called a moat. Because when you think of moats, you usually think of them surrounding castles, not gorillas.)

"No," I say. "What are you going to do to that gorilla?"

"Allow me to enlighten you," he says. "I'm going to open up a can of whup-butt on him."

"Not a can of whup-butt," I gasp.

"That's right," says Hambone. "You mess with me, you get a whupping—can-of-whup-butt style."

(Speaking of a can of whup-butt, Hambone once opened one up on this little poodle who tried to sniff his butt. Which is kind of funny if you think about it—opening up a can of whup-butt because someone tried to sniff your butt. That's a lot of butts. But that's what Hambone did. I think the poodle was just saying hello. Hambone didn't agree. Let's just say he didn't say hi back.)

Hambone walks right up to the edge of the moat.

He looks around the clearing at all the gorillas, trying to figure out which one is the one he wants.

"It's hard with them all being asleep," he says.

"Maybe we should come back later," I say.

Hambone ignores me. "Is that the one?" he says, pointing to a gorilla asleep on top of a fallen tree.

"I don't know," I say. "It could be."

(To be honest, I don't really remember which gorilla threw the dirt at him. But it was definitely a big one. And the one sleeping on the fallen tree is big. Real big.)

"Here, gorilla, gorilla. Here, gorilla," says Hambone.

The gorilla doesn't move.

Hambone leans over the moat and screams, "Wake up, you stupid idiot! It's go time."

"I don't think screaming at him is going to work," I say.

"Oh, yeah," he says. "Well, if he doesn't wake up soon, I'll tell you what's going to work: me swimming across this moat and opening up a can of whup-butt on him."

I can tell Hambone is deadly serious.

Which makes me think: Uh-oh. This isn't going to end well.

Chapter Three

Hambone takes off his collar.

"Here," he says, handing it to me. "Hold this. I don't want it to get wet."

"What are you doing?" I say.

"Just what I said I was going to do," he says. "If that gorilla thinks I'm playing around, he's sadly mistaken."

"You're seriously going to swim over there? How? Doggie paddle?"

"Very funny."

Hambone gets set to dive in.

"Wait a second," I say. "Look over there."

I'm pointing to this guy who has suddenly appeared out of nowhere.

"What about him?" says Hambone.

"Who is he?"

"He's not a big, stupid moron gorilla," he says. "So I don't care."

"He's not a zoo employee, I know that," I say. "They have to wear those blue T-shirts with their name stitched on the front pocket. You know the ones."

"Yeah. Stupidest T-shirts ever. Why do they have a bald eagle on the back? I've never seen a bald eagle at this zoo. Just bald guys."

"Well, whoever he is, he sure is weird looking."

And when I say weird looking, I mean weird looking. His hair is a bunch of silvery-white strands. It looks as if somebody plopped a handful of tinsel on top of his head. He's wearing green-tinted sunglasses, a red bow tie, black gloves that go all the way up to his shoulder, a white lab coat that goes all the way down to his knees, and black sneakers.

I start laughing.

"What's so funny?" says Hambone.

"I was just thinking about these really bad science-fiction movies my older brother makes we watch late at night," I say. "They're so bad they're funny. And there's always this crazy mad-scientist guy in them. That's what this weird-looking guy reminds me of."

"Mad scientist? You think he's a mad scientist?"

"If he is, he needs a name. All the ones in the movies I've seen have funny-sounding names. Like Evil Doctor Baron Von Frickenstein. Or Evil Doctor Siegfried Van Der Dorff. I think I shall call this weird-looking guy Evil Doctor Crazy Gorilla."

"That's pretty good," says Hambone.

Just then, Evil Doctor Crazy Gorilla looks over in our direction.

"Quick," I say, diving behind a trash barrel. "Before he sees us."

I hear Hambone sigh.

"What are you doing?" he says, walking over to me.

I look up at him. "Obviously I'm ducking for cover."

"Seriously?" he says. "He wasn't even looking at us."

"It sure looked like he was. And who knows what Evil Doctor Crazy Gorilla might do if he knows we are watching him?"

Hambone sniffs. "Get up, you moron," he says. "Nothing is going to happen."

"How can you be so sure?" I say.

"Because he's not a mad scientist. I bet he's just some homeless guy who sleeps in the zoo. He's harmless."

"Says you. But what if he really is a mad scientist?"

"What if he's really a ballerina?" says Hambone, being sarcastic. "Or a magical being from the fairy planet Tinkerdust? I mean, he could really be anything. Right? So why don't we just take it down a notch. See what this guy is up to before jumping to any conclusions."

"OK," I say, getting up from behind the trash barrel. "But you should be warned. If he really is a mad scientist, they don't take kindly to people messing with their evil plans. I can tell you that."

"Look at me; I'm shaking," he says.

I look at him.

He's not shaking.

"Don't say I didn't warn you," I say.

We watch as Evil Doctor Crazy Gorilla goes over to the big gorilla sleeping on the fallen tree.

"This should be interesting," I say. "Doesn't he know it's not smart to wake a sleeping gorilla? Or is it a sleeping bear?"

"Shh," says Hambone. "I'm trying to watch here."

"Nobody's stopping you."

Evil Doctor Crazy Gorilla gently nudges the big gorilla. It doesn't wake up. It just stretches and turns over on its other side.

"Boy, that's one sleepy gorilla," I say.

"Let me go over there," says Hambone. "I'll wake him up."

Evil Doctor Crazy Gorilla keeps nudging the big gorilla. It stretches and turns over again but this time falls off the tree in the process. Thud! Right on its head.

"That's one way to do it," I say.

The big gorilla doesn't wake up happy. It starts pounding its chest, making angry gorilla noises that sound like gorilla swears: SON-OF-A-OO-AH-AH!

Hambone sniffs.

"Oh, poor wittle gowilla," he says. "All mad because he bonked his wittle head. Boo-hoo."

But that's not how I would describe the way the big gorilla is acting. Mad is not a strong enough word—he's going ballistic.

"Evil Doctor Crazy Gorilla better get out of there while he still can," I say.

But he doesn't.

Instead, he nonchalantly walks over and stands face to face with the big gorilla.

"Is he out of his mind?" I say. "Or does he have a death wish?"

Neither, it turns out.

I keep watching as Evil Doctor Crazy Gorilla stands motionless in front of the big gorilla. Not moving a single muscle. Not even an eyelash as he stares into the big gorilla's eyes.

It's as if he is a gorilla whisperer. Attempting to communicate calming thoughts without speaking. And it works. The big gorilla eventually calms down.

"That was amazing," I say. "Maybe I should start calling him Evil Doctor Crazy Gorilla whisperer."

"Don't be stupid," says Hambone. "What he did wasn't all that great."

I think it was. I mean, Evil Doctor Crazy Gorilla definitely has a way with gorillas. They listen to him.

Wait a second.

Is that what his evil plan is? Does it involve the gorillas? Is that why he is in the clearing in the first place?

I share my ideas with Hambone.

He scoffs.

"I think it makes sense," I say.

"I'll tell you what makes sense," says Hambone. "This guy doesn't have special gorilla powers. He probably just really loves gorillas. I bet he's the president of the Gorilla Fan Club of America."

"No way," I say. "I mean, look at him. Look how he's now saying something to the big gorilla. What do you think it is?"

"Probably how much he loves him and how nobody understands how hard it is to be a gorilla, but he knows, blah blah blah."

Whatever he said, it makes the big gorilla lean its head back and open its mouth like a baby bird about to get its food from its mother.

"Feeding time?" I say.

Evil Doctor Crazy Gorilla reaches into the front pocket of his lab coat and takes out one of those old-fashioned medicine bottles. He removes the cork stopper. Greenish smoke billows out.

Oh-my-shnippies!

"Look at that," I say. "See? He's got some sort of potion there. I knew it. He really is a mad scientist."

"Yeah, yeah," says Hambone. "That doesn't prove anything."

"It sure does," I say. "In all the movies I've seen, potion equals mad scientist. So I've been right all along."

"Whatever," he says dismissively.

Hambone isn't a big fan of patting you on the back. He is a big fan of you patting him on the back, however. Which is fine. It doesn't have to go both ways. I'm just glad we now know who this guy is. Before us stands Evil Doctor Crazy Gorilla: mad scientist.

Speaking of which, he carefully turns the old-fashioned medicine bottle upside down and pours some of the green potion into the big gorilla's mouth.

Nothing happens.

Or maybe I should say something does happen, but only after a few seconds. Suddenly the big gorilla looks different.

The more I look at him, the more he doesn't look like any gorilla I know. It's like how my mom doesn't look like any mom I know when I forget to flush the toilet. She looks different. Like she wants to flush me down the toilet. And that's how the big gorilla looks now.

"This can't be good," I say.

And I'm right.

The big gorilla starts convulsing. As if it's having a seizure. Then, just like that, its body stops convulsing and goes motionless. All stiff like.

"I think whatever Evil Doctor Crazy Gorilla gave that big gorilla just killed him," I say.

I wish.

The reason I wish is because of what happens next. After a few minutes of lying stiff as a board, the gorilla gets up. Its body suddenly changes, morphing from a gorilla into a...into a...no...this can't be happening. Its eyes turn bloodshot and bulge out of its head. Its jaw drops open, and its canine teeth grow into huge yellow fangs. Its chest sinks in, and its arms and legs shrivel up into deformed limbs. Its fur turns from black to gray and sags off his bones. Blood dribbles out of a gash opening up on its forehead. The gorilla isn't just some ordinary gorilla anymore. No. I can't believe I'm going to tell you this. But now it's a...*zombie* gorilla.

"Ah, I think we should probably go now," I say.

"Are you kidding?" says Hambone. "I came here to open up a can of whup-butt on that big gorilla who threw dirt at me, and that's what I'm going to do."

"Even if it's now a zombie?" I say. "I mean, that's what going on here, right? What Evil Doctor Crazy Gorilla's plan is? I mean, it couldn't be more obvious. He's turning gorillas into zombie gorillas."

"That's even better," says Hambone. "I hate zombies just as much as I hate gorillas."

It's true. He does.

"Well, be that as it may," I say. "Zombies and gorillas—those are two things I don't ever want to say in the same sentence. We should have been gone ten seconds ago."

Hambone stands up straight and crosses his arms over his chest. He's not going anywhere.

"Fine," I say. "Stay here if you want. I'm going."

But I don't move. I can't move. It's as if my legs are stuck in mud. Or worse—quicksand. And it feels like the more I try to move, the more I'm getting sucked down deeper into the quicksand.

Being in such close proximity to a zombie gorilla will do that to you, believe me.

"You still here?" says Hambone.

"My legs are stuck."

"Stuck?" Hambone smirks and then starts flapping his arms. "Bock. Bock."

"You're calling me a chicken?" I say.

"Well, aren't you?" he says. "I mean, look at you. You're so scared you can't even move."

"Oh, forgive me for being so scared it's like I'm stuck in quicksand. What was I thinking? I should be jumping up and down shouting, 'Yeah! Zombie gorillas!' at the top of my lungs. So sorry. There must be something wrong with me."

"Well," says Hambone, "if you really want to know—"

"Wait," I say. "What is he doing now?"

Evil Doctor Crazy Gorilla goes over to each of the sleeping gorillas, gently nudging them awake and giving them some of the green potion. They also turn into zombie gorillas.

"Are you still staying here, Hambone?" I say. "It's not just one, it's about thirty zombie gorillas now."

"You bet," he says. "Now it's getting interesting."

The zombie gorillas circle around one another. At first it looks as if they're just playing. They hoot and beat their chests and slap at the ground. But then they charge at one another, chomping out chunks of one another's flesh.

"Holy moly," I say. "These must be some serious flesh-eating zombie gorillas if they're willing to eat the flesh of another zombie gorilla."

Evil Doctor Crazy Gorilla does his gorilla whisperer stuff again. It works. The zombie gorillas stop attacking one another and slowly swarm around Evil Doctor Crazy Gorilla, staggering as they knuckle walk. Some linger at the moat and spit out their chewed-up bits of flesh into the water, changing the color from blue to red.

"Eww," I say. "That's gross."

"I think it's kind of funny," says Hambone.

"Funny?" I say. "The only thing that's going to be funny is how fast I get the heck out of here."

Hambone gives me a look.

"What?" I say.

"Your legs are stuck, remember?"

He's right. Darn this quicksand.

But I have to get out of here somehow. There's no telling what Evil Doctor Crazy Gorilla and these zombie gorillas are up to.

I look around for help. Maybe some of the workers have shown up by now—the zoo should be opening soon. And if they have, maybe they'll see me and come and rescue me before it's too late. But I don't see any zoo workers.

What I do see is Evil Doctor Crazy Gorilla doing more of his gorilla-whisperer stuff on the zombie gorillas again. And then, as if everything that has happened up to this point weren't messed up enough, what happens next is even more messed up.

The zombie gorillas arrange themselves into rows. One in front of the other. Like an army amassing at the border of a country they are going to invade. Which makes Evil Doctor Crazy Gorilla the general in charge of the troops—waiting for the right moment to give the order to attack.

I look at Hambone.

"Quicksand or no quicksand, I have to get out of here," I say. "It's now or never."

I grab my right leg with both hands and pull as hard as I can.

Ffsuuuuuuuuup!

I free my right leg from the grip of the quicksand. I do the same with my left leg. Before I know it, I'm on solid ground and running as fast as I can. As far away from Evil Doctor Crazy Gorilla and those zombie gorillas as my little legs will take me.

Chapter Four

"**H**elloooooo. Hellooooooooo in there. Come out, come out, wherever you are. Hellooooooooooooo!"

I don't answer Hambone. Why not? Because I know what's coming next. It's not a can of whoop-butt he's going to open up on me, but worse. He's going to open up a can of busting-chops.

"Go away," I say. "Leave me alone."

"Aw," says Hambone, using his best baby voice. "What's the matter, little Peas? Did the big bad zombie gorillas make you want to go 'wee, wee, wee' all the way home?"

See what I mean? Busting chops. When it comes to busting chops, Hambone is the best. They should give him a medal. Call it the Royal Order of Busting Chops.

"That's not very cool," I say. "What if I was truly traumatized by what I saw? I could be scarred for life. You wouldn't be busting my chops then, would you?"

"Maybe," says Hambone.

"Really? Thanks a bunch."

"My pleasure."

"Not that I hope it makes you feel bad," I say. "But I wouldn't bust your chops if you were truly traumatized."

"You couldn't even if you wanted to," he says.

"Why not?"

"Because I'd report you to the ASPCA quicker than you can say Jack Robinson," he says. "Busting my chops? That's cruelty to animals."

Hambone laughs.

I have to give him credit—he is the best.

But that doesn't mean I'm not annoyed by it.

"Go away!" I yell.

"Come on," says Hambone. "Stop being such a baby. I promise no more busting your chops. Just come on out of there, OK?"

I reluctantly crawl out from under my back porch.

"I'm surprised to see you here," I say.

"Why's that?" says Hambone.

"I thought you were having so much fun with those zombie gorillas," I say, still a little annoyed. "I thought you might want to stay with them and roast marshmallows over a nice, warm fire. Maybe sing 'Kumbaya' while you're at it."

"That sounds like fun."

"So why aren't you still there?"

"Because I missed you," he says, giving me a big hug. "You don't know how hard it was for me to be away from you. You're my best friend."

I can't tell if he's still busting my chops. But even still, the hug is nice. If you really want to know the truth, seeing those gorillas turn into zombie gorillas scared the you-know-what out of me. (Think the one with the two e's.)

"You're my best friend, too," I say. "But you start in on me again, and I go right back to where I was. I swear."

"Don't worry," says Hambone. "No more busting chops."

"Good," I say. "So what do we do now?"

"What do you mean?"

"Seriously?" I say, giving him a look. "Evil Doctor Crazy Gorilla is turning ordinary gorillas into zombie gorillas, and you're giving me 'What do you mean?' You saw the way those zombie gorillas were maneuvering—getting into tactical formation. What if they're going to attack—like right now? Is that Evil Doctor Crazy Gorilla's plan? Using an army of zombie gorillas to take over the world? I don't know about you, but I don't want to live in a world ruled by zombie gorillas."

"Zombies shmombies," he says. "I'm so sick of hearing about zombies."

One of Hambone's rants is coming on. He does this. So get ready.

"Zombie this and zombie that," he continues. "Everywhere you look—there's a zombie. Zombie movies. Zombie TV shows. Zombie books. Zombie video games. I'm surprised there isn't a zombie cereal. Just think of it: the cereal pieces could be shaped like severed heads. Yum, yum, yum. I'm surprised some marketing genius hasn't thought of it already. I tell you. They think we're morons. They think that just because some zombie thing was popular, they can just give us all zombies all the time. Zombies are cool—if you're seven. Then you get over it. They are so five years ago. But no. Everybody is still jumping on the zombie bandwagon. And they're going to ride it for every penny it's worth. Greedy low-lifes. It's disgusting. Forcing zombies down our throats. It makes me want to puke on every zombie I see. Just for being a zombie."

Hambone stops. He's worked himself up so much he's exhausted. His tongue lolls out of his mouth. This also happens at the end of one of his rants.

I wait for him to cool down.

(By the way, I don't agree with what Hambone said. I think zombies are cool. Way, way cool. And I'm ten.)

"What a day," says Hambone. "All I wanted was to open up a can of whup-butt on that gorilla that threw dirt at me, and now this—zombie gorillas. Boy, could it get any worse? I mean, did I do something to somebody in a previous life? Are they looking at me and laughing? Pointing and saying, 'Ha! Ha! You hate gorillas and zombies? Well, guess what? We put the two together just for you—have fun!'? But I guess I should look on the bright side. I have a chance to open up a can of whup-butt on the two things I hate most in the world. This might actually be a pretty good day after all. So what do you say? What do we do now? Let's do this. Let's go open a can of whup-but on some zombie gorillas."

"I don't think that's such a good idea," I say.

"Why not?" he says. "We have to do something. You said yourself that they looked like they were getting ready to attack. Maybe even trying to take over the world. So we'll give them a little can of whup-butt action, and that will be that. No more zombie gorillas."

"How big is your can of whup-butt?" I say, exasperated.

"What does that have to do with anything?" he says.

"We're not just dealing with one zombie gorilla here," I say. "There were what, maybe thirty or so of them? And that's just the beginning."

"The beginning?"

"Yeah, the beginning. That's the thing about zombies you don't know because you're too busy hating them. But I know a lot about them. I'm somewhat of an expert. Thanks to my brother, I've seen about a million zombie movies."

"I bet all you saw was his butt," says Hambone out of the corner of his mouth.

"What was that?" I say.

"I thought you said he sat on you and made you watch."

"Well, I could still see the TV. And what I saw was zombies, zombies everywhere. So I know that once these zombie gorillas start eating people's flesh, those people will also turn into zombie gorillas, and before you know it—zombie gorillas, zombie gorillas everywhere. So unless you have the biggest can of whup-butt in the world, I think we should go get some help."

"Help?" says Hambone, raising an eyebrow. "Who's going to help us?"

"Plenty of people," I say.

"People are useless," he says.

"Oh, yeah? What about the police?"

"Useless."

"How about the workers at the zoo?"

"Useless."

"Parents?"

"Useless."

"Teachers?"

"Beyond useless."

"Friends?"

Hambone shakes his head. "Contrary to public opinion, I do know a little something about zombies. But since you're the zombie expert, you tell me: What happens to most people in a zombie movie?"

"I told you. They get turned into zombies. In like the first ten minutes of the movie. That's why—"

Hambone cuts me off. "So in other words, they're basically useless. Unless you want to go to a zombie for help, which I don't think you want to do."

"No. Of course not."

"So doesn't that mean it's just you and me, pal? The two of us? The two amigos? Saving the world from the attack of the zombie gorillas?"

"Yeah, I guess so." I hate to admit it, but he's right. I mean, every movie has to have a hero. Somebody people can root for. Somebody who saves the day. So I guess that's me and Hambone. We are the heroes of this story. But boy, what a depressing thought. Heroes sometimes die, you know.

"Hey, cheer up, buttercup," says Hambone, coming over to me and putting his arm around my shoulder. "This isn't going to be so bad. Zombies shmombies. It'll be over before you know it. And then, guess what? We'll be famous. We'll be the guys who rid the world of zombie gorillas. Just think, people will give us money, Lamborghinis, diamonds, whatever we want."

"You know what I really want?" I say.

"What?"

"I want an ax or a pick. Not a can of whup-butt—that isn't going to cut it. If we're going to do this, if we're going to stop these zombie gorillas, we need something to smash their heads in to get to their brains. That's how you stop them for real."

"That's the spirit," says Hambone, lightly shaking my shoulders. "So what do you say we go to your dad's shed and get us some gardening tools?"

My dad's this big gardener. Likes to spend his weekends gardening. So he bought this shed a couple of years ago to keep all his tools in. The shed is enormous. It looks like a miniature house right in our backyard.

"I don't know why you guys put me in that puny doghouse," says Hambone, stopping in front of the shed. "I should be living here. Boy, I bet a family of oompa loompas could live in here comfortably."

I go to open the shed door. But there's a combination lock on it.

"When did your dad put that on?" says Hambone.

"I don't know," I say. "And I also don't know the combination. This isn't good. My dad doesn't get home from work until five o'clock. That's like twenty hours from now in zombie gorilla time."

"Don't worry," he says. "I can pick that thing in like thirty seconds flat."

"You know how to pick a lock? I didn't know you knew how to do that."

"I know all sorts of things."

"I can't pick anything."

"Don't sell yourself short," he says. "You're an expert at picking your nose."

"Hey, that's not fair," I say. "I can't help it if I have bad sinuses. It's genetic. Blame my parents."

Hambone sniffs. Then he goes over to our recycle bin on the back porch. He rummages through it and comes out with a soda can. He bites into the can, tearing off a jagged piece of aluminum. He folds the jagged piece over into the shape of a triangle. Then he folds it again into a smaller triangle.

"That should do it," says Hambone.

"What should do what?" I say.

"Just watch," he says. He goes over to the combination lock. He sticks the aluminum triangle piece he made into the curved metal bar. He takes it out. Then he sticks it back in again, only harder. Kind of like he's trying to jam it into the curved metal bar. He keeps jamming it until—boing! The lock opens.

"That was amazing," I say.

"Save your applause," says Hambone, walking into the shed.

"I think what we're looking for is hanging up on the walls," I say, following right behind him.

"Holy smokes," he says. "Are you kidding me with this place?"

Nobody's kidding anybody. Except maybe my dad. The reason I say this is because we don't find any gardening tools at first. Instead we find a flat-screen TV, a mini-fridge stocked with beer, a lounge chair with compartments filed with potato chips and beef jerky—all hooked up to a generator.

"This isn't a shed," says Hambone. "This is a man cave."

"No wonder he spends all his time in here," I say.

"I have to hand it to your dad," he says. "I didn't think he had it in him. But what a perfect scam. He had me fooled."

"Me, too," I say. "Wow, I can't believe he's scamming us."

"Maybe he's not scamming at all," he says. "Maybe he's a superhero—Couch Potato Man. And he has the power to sit on his butt all day and not spend time with his family. Instead of up, up, and away, it's sit, sit, and veg."

"That doesn't make me feel better," I say.

In one corner of the shed, we actually do find an ax and a pick shovel. So maybe I can give my dad some credit for at least keeping up appearances.

"Which one do you want?" says Hambone.

I take the ax and give Hambone the pick shovel. Then we lock the shed back up on our way out.

The ax feels kind of heavy in my hand. I'm not really sure I'll be able to wield it when the time comes.

I practice swinging it a couple times.

It drops out of my hand.

Not because I lost my grip but because my grip lost me. What I mean is, this sudden shock zaps my body, a bolt of electricity causing all my muscles to suddenly stop working.

Hambone notices this.

"What's the matter?" he says.

I try to speak, but I can't. The shock has worn off, but for some reason it has left the muscles in my face useless. All I can do is try to act out what I want to say. Like charades.

"OK," says Hambone, picking up on what's happening. "How many words?"

I put up two fingers.

"First word?" he says.

I stick my arms straight out.

"You're tired."

I shake my head. I start groaning.

"You're tired, and you feel sick to your stomach."

I shake my head. I put up two fingers again.

"OK," he says. "Second word."

I hop on one leg and then the other, doing this little jig-like dance.

"You have a hot foot?" he says. "No. You'd be jumping up and down on only one foot. Two hot feet? No. You're stepping on hot coals? How about ants in your pants?"

Seriously? I shake my head. Then I try to think of another clue. I start pounding my chest as I do my jig-like dance.

"You have heartburn?" He keeps guessing. "Indigestion? Wait—I got it? You're choking on a piece of food? No? What?"

Maybe it's because of Hambone's astounding stupidity. Or maybe it's because my face muscles are no longer useless. But I can speak again.

"Look behind you!" I scream.

Hambone turns around.

Standing right in front of him is a squad of zombie gorillas.

CHAPTER FIVE

I try to remember the last time I saw Hambone falling from that high in the air.

I think it was when he fell out of the tree in Mrs. Madigan's yard.

He was chasing Mrs. Madigan's cat. That cat was pretty smart. She went all the way to the top of the tree figuring Hambone wouldn't have the guts to follow. But he did. And as he was just about to sink his teeth into little Fluffylufugus, he slipped and fell, plummeting to the ground. When he hit, he sat up all dazed like. And I swear I could see little birdies circling around his head. Just like in the cartoons.

I wonder if I'll see them again when he lands this time.

Wait a second. I shouldn't be thinking that.

I should be horrified that just a moment ago one of the zombie gorillas grabbed Hambone and flung him about thirty feet into the air.

He's on his way down now.

Three. Two. One.

THUD!

Hambone sits up.

Nope. No little birdies this time.

But he's definitely dazed.

"Holly mother of..." says Hambone. But he doesn't have the chance to finish his sentence. That's because another zombie gorilla knocks him to the ground and starts stomping on his back.

"I...could...use...a...little...help...here," gasps Hambone in between stomps.

I reach down for my ax. It feels like it weighs a ton. With every muscle in my body straining, I lift the ax over my head and—SMASH! Right down on the zombie gorilla's oversized noggin.

Its skull cracks open like a watermelon dropped from a tall building onto the sidewalk below. But instead of yummy, pulpy-pink stuff splattering everywhere, it's just the opposite. This oozy mixture of brain and snot and pus splatters all over me. On my clothes. And little bitty chunks land on my face.

I wipe off what I can, but it's not good enough.

The smell. It's worse than the Gorilla Kingdom smell. It's as bad as if a million gorilla corpses were putrefying in the Gorilla Kingdom.

Makes you lose your appetite smelling that smell, believe me. You might even lose something else—like your lunch.

I try not to breathe.

But I have to. Obviously.

"Don't just stand there," says Hambone, shaking off the pain. "There's more where that one came from."

He's right.

"Watch out," I say.

Another zombie gorilla lurches at Hambone. But he thinks fast. He squats down and whips his leg out, chopping the legs out from under the zombie gorilla.

"Wow!" I say. "That was pretty cool."

"I'll give you an autograph later," says Hambone. "But for now, why don't you give me that ax."

I toss it over to him.

"Remember, you have to get to his brain," I say.

Hambone does just that.

More of that oozy mixture splatters out.

"You're going to want to hold your nose," I say. "That stuff reeks."

Hambone tosses the ax back to me. "You're going to want to hold that," he says, nodding toward something behind me. "Zombie gorilla—ten o'clock."

I turn and swing my ax at the same time, hoping to make contact with whatever zombie gorilla is there.

But I only make contact with air. What the...?

I look down.

Oh, so that's why. It's a baby zombie gorilla.

Awww. How cute.

But it isn't cute what that baby zombie gorilla does next.

It smiles and then grabs my...it...um...well...how do I put this politely? I could...but. Um...OK...I guess I'll just come out and say it: it grabs my private parts.

"Hey, that's not fair grabbing a kid down there," I say, my voice suddenly high-pitched and squeaky.

"All's fair in love and war with flesh-eating zombie gorillas," says Hambone, rushing up to help me.

He gives the baby zombie gorilla a forearm shiver to the neck, sending it tumbling backward.

"Take that," he says. He holds out his hand, pretending he's clutching a can. And then with the other hand, he pretends to lift back the tab on the can he's clutching.

"PsssssCH!"

"What's that?" I say.

"I just opened up a can of whup-butt," he says. He stares at the baby zombie gorilla on the ground. "How do you like me now?"

Obviously in all the excitement, Hambone forgot what I told him—a can of whup-butt isn't going to have any effect on a zombie gorilla. Even a baby zombie gorilla.

Speaking of which, that baby zombie gorilla Hambone knocked backward is now up on its feet, dusting itself off. It turns sideways, spreads its legs farther apart, and bends its knees. Girding itself for a fight. Then it waves Hambone to come at it.

"Is it challenging me?" says Hambone.

"I think so," I say.

"It's challenging me," he says again. "Unbelievable."

"Remember," I say. "Pick shovel—not a can of whup-butt."

Luckily, the pick shovel is within Hambone's reach. He bends down and picks it up.

"Here little baby zombie gorilla," he says. "Come to Hambone and get your brains smashed in."

He swings the pick shovel around his body, passing it from hand to hand as it goes around and around. Like that Bruce Lee kung-fu guy with the nunchucks.

(My brother forces me to watch kung-fu movies, too.)

Then Hambone passes the pick shovel over and under each arm. Again and again. Getting faster each time he does it.

(He's doing some serious kung-fu stuff now. Bruce Lee has nothing on Hambone.)

The baby zombie gorilla doesn't know what to do. It's torn. Should it wait for Hambone to come at it, or is it going to have to go at Hambone? It decides to go at Hambone. But I don't think it really wants to. It gingerly steps closer to Hambone. Like a kid on the beach testing the ocean with his toes to see how cold the water is. It steps even closer but then jumps back when the pick shovel almost whacks it.

"What's a matter, baby zombie gorilla?" says Hambone. "I'm not going to hurt you. I'm just going to bash your brains in."

The baby zombie gorilla grunts.

Hambone sniffs. "Come on," he says. "Come closer again. I dare you."

More grunting.

"What if I do this?" says Hambone, resting the pick shovel on his shoulder.

"I wouldn't do that if I were you," I warn.

Seeing this as his chance to get at Hambone, the baby zombie gorilla opens its mouth wide and lunges forward.

"WATCHAAAW," yells Hambone as he whacks the baby zombie gorilla right between the eyes.

The baby zombie gorilla crumples to the ground with the pick shovel still stuck in its head.

"Did you bait him on purpose?" I say, not really sure.

"I had to do something," says Hambone. "I wasn't going to wait around all day."

He stands on the baby zombie gorilla's neck and pries the pick shovel loose. It takes some doing, but he finally gets it.

"Right behind you!" I shout, pointing.

"Hwaieeeee-YAAHHHHHH," yells Hambone as he turns and whacks and smashes every zombie gorilla that comes near him—Bruce Lee style.

"WOOOOOOOO-ooooOOOO-WAHHHHHHHHH!" I yell. Why not? It's working for Hambone. The only difference is Hambone is really good at wielding his pick shovel. I'm not so good. Every time I try to pass the shovel round my body, it ends up hitting me in the forehead.

Doink!

Hurts like a...but that's not the worst part. The worst part of it is the zombie gorillas think I'm a fool.

(It's bad enough that every kid at my school thinks that, but now zombie gorillas as well? Just shoot me now.)

"What are you doing over there, Peas?" says Hambone.

"I'm doing my best, but they're laughing at me," I say. "See? They have these big smiles on their faces."

"I think that means they like you," he says, smiling.

(Now is definitely not the time for busting chops.)

I smash one zombie gorilla in the head and then another and another.

"How many are there?" I say.

"I don't know," says Hambone. "Why don't you ask them? Maybe invite them to stay for tea while you're at it."

"I'm just saying."

"Well, stop saying and start smashing."

I do.

But it's weird. I could swear one of the zombie gorillas I smashed is the same one I smashed earlier. The same one whose brain chunks are still on my clothes.

Could it really be the same zombie gorilla? Is that even possible?

I have to know. It's killing me. I need scientifically verifiable proof. (When I grow up, I'm going to be a scientist—I have a keen scientific mind.)

I decide to conduct an experiment.

"Hambone, do you want to do me a favor here?" I say. I figure I can get Hambone to taste one of the chunks on my clothes and then compare the taste with a chunk of brain from the zombie gorilla I just smashed. Gross? Not to Hambone. He licks his butt.

"I'm kind of busy at the moment," he says, whacking and smashing zombie gorillas. "Whatever it is, can it wait?"

Unfortunately, no, it can't. I'm going to have to do it, I guess. After all, it's in the name of science. So I taste the two different chunks of brains.

Yup. They taste the same.

Holy moly. You know what this means, don't you? These zombie gorillas are somehow coming back to life even after getting their brains smashed in. They're regenerating! If that's the case, how do you stop them? There is no stopping them.

Oh-my-shnobbies!

The world will be theirs in no time.

I don't have time to worry about that.

Another squadron of zombie gorillas invades our backyard. A blitzkrieg of gray fur and yellow fangs seemingly coming from all directions. Over the grass. From out under the porch. Some swinging down from tree branches. Some even jumping off the roof of my dad's shed. All headed in our direction. If me and Hambone don't get out of here, the next sentence you're going to read will be one describing the excruciating pain caused by a zombie gorilla biting off your flesh. Owww!

"Retreat! Retreat!" I yell.

Luckily, Hambone agrees with me.

CHAPTER SIX

As we're running away across Franklin Park, I hear this sound overhead.

I look up.

I don't believe my eyes. It's a World War I fighter plane. The only World War I fighter plane I know of belongs to Mr. Oswalt. He's this crazy old guy in our neighborhood who thinks he's a flying ace in World War I. Kind of like Snoopy thinking he's battling his archenemy, the Red Baron. But Mr. Oswalt isn't sitting on top of his doghouse claiming he's flying a Sopwith Camel—he went out and bought a real one.

And that's the plane now heading directly toward us.

Oh-my-shneggies!

The upper and lower wings look like giant knife blades. The propeller, the blade in a blender. That's a lot of blades.

Which isn't good. Not if you want to stay in one piece.

We dive to the ground and cover our heads with our hands—just in time.

WHOOSH!

The plane flies over, trailing a wave of air that nearly lifts us off the ground.

"What's he doing?" says Hambone. "Is he trying to kill us?"

The plane circles around and comes back in our direction.

"I don't know," I say. "But let's not wait around and find out."

We get up and start running—as fast as our little legs will take us.

Ouch!

I turn my ankle in a sinkhole and fall, smacking my face right into the ground.

That's going to leave a big mark.

"Get up," says Hambone, turning to look at me but not stopping.

I can't get up. To be honest with you, I'm a little dazed. Like cartoon-seeing-birdies dazed. Yup. There they are now.

"Come back, pretty birdies," I say.

Hambone turns and sees me still on the ground, so he stops.

"Here, pretty birdies," I say.

"What are you talking about?" says Hambone, rushing to my aid. He picks me up, puts me on his shoulder, and starts running again.

"Don't you see the pretty birdies?" I say.

"I don't see any birdies," he says. "All I see is a plane heading straight for us."

He runs faster.

WHOOSH!

The plane passes just inches above our heads.

The wave of air this time causes Hambone to stumble and fall. When he lands on the ground, he lets go of me, and I tumble forward a few yards more. Which isn't the most wonderful experience considering I'm still feeling a little dazed.

"Look at the pretty birdies," I say.

"Enough with the birdies," says Hambone.

"But they're so pretty."

"Enough!"

I snap out of it.

Just in time to watch the plane as it lands on the soccer field, does a pirouette, and taxis right up to us.

"What's he going to do now?" I say.

"Probably try to run us over," says Hambone. "He's crazy."

Mr. Oswalt turns off the engine and climbs out of the cockpit.

He's dressed in full flying-ace regalia: leather bomber jacket, aviator helmet, goggles, and a red scarf.

"I heard a great deal of commotion in the neighborhood," says Mr. Oswalt. "Are the Germans on the attack again?"

"Germans?" I say. "They aren't Germans, Mr. Oswalt. They're zombie gorillas."

"Now, now, young man," says Mr. Oswalt. "I know there's a tendency in the heat of battle to disparage the enemy. But it's not becoming a gentleman to resort to name-calling. Actually, it's downright uncivilized."

"Boy, this old guy really is off his rocker," whispers Hambone.

I elbow him in the ribs.

"I'm just saying," whispers Hambone. "Besides, you don't need to elbow me. Even if I were to jump up and down reciting the Gettysburg Address in front of ole Mr. Out-of-of His-Mind here, he'd still wouldn't suspect a thing. Our secret is safe with us."

He's right. But still. We don't want to push it.

"Where is the enemy now?" says Mr. Oswalt.

"Back there somewhere," I say, pointing over my shoulder. "But I hope we've lost them. The last thing I want to see right now is a zombie gorilla."

"Language, young man," says Mr. Oswalt. "Remember your language."

"But you don't understand," I say. "These zombie gorillas...er...um...I mean, the Germans—if they catch up to us—are going to eat our flesh off."

"I got an idea," says Hambone, pulling me off to the side so Mr. Oswalt won't hear. "Ask him to go back up in his plane and shoot at the zombie gorillas for us."

"What's that going to do?" I say. "You have to smash their brains in, remember?"

"And how do you smash their brains in?" says Hambone.

"You need a weapon," I say.

"Exactly," says Hambone. "Do you see any around here?"

Uh-oh. We dropped the ax and pick shovel back at our house when we retreated.

"That plane is the best weapon we have right now," says Hambone. "At the very least, he'll keep them occupied so we can find new ones."

"OK," I say. "I'll give it a try."

"If you want some help, just let me know," he says.

"No," I say. "I got this." (If there's one thing I know how to do, it's talk to crazy old people. I've had a lot of practice with my grandfather. He's even crazier than Mr. Oswalt. How much crazier? My grandfather thinks he's the King of Waffle Land and I'm his loyal subject, Bob.)

"Wow, that sure is a neat plane you have there, Mr. Oswalt," I say. "I bet you could shoot down a lot of Germans with that plane."

Mr. Oswalt stands taller.

"I have forty-nine confirmed kills," he says, beaming. "Of course, when you are as skilled as I am, your fellow aces get jealous. Did you know they tried to steal my Distinguished Flying Crosses? How dare they? Each one was awarded personally to me by His Majesty King George V."

Now it's Hambone's turn to elbow me in the ribs. He points insistently to the plane.

"I know," I say. "But it takes time. You can't just come out and ask. You don't know how they might react." (One time my grandfather threw waffles at my head because he was mad at me for forgetting that Waffle Land was once ruled by the evil Eggo Elves.)

"What was that, young man?" says Mr. Oswalt. "Are you saying something? Speak up."

"Right," I say. "Sorry. Um...what kind of gas mileage do you get in a plane like that?"

"I have a range of about three hundred miles," says Mr. Oswalt, "depending on the wind, of course."

"Cool," I say. "My dad gets about fifty miles to the gallon in his hybrid."

Hambone howls.

"What?" I say.

"Seriously?" he whispers. "Well, you can stay here chitchatting with Commander Cuckoo Bird if you want, but I'm not going to let a perfectly good plane go to waste. See you."

"Come back here," I say.

I watch Hambone sneak around Mr. Oswalt. When he makes it to the plane unnoticed, he smiles, waves good-bye, and jumps into the cockpit.

"Um, excuse me, Mr. Oswalt," I say. "I'll be right back. Why don't you stand guard and let us know if you see any Germans approaching."

"Excellent idea," says Mr. Oswalt, snapping to attention and saluting me.

I salute him back and then head over to Hambone.

"What are you doing?" I say.

"What does it look like I'm doing?" he says. "I'm going to get out of here before those zombie gorillas show up."

"Come, on. Get out of there. What if Mr. Oswalt catches you?"

"Are you kidding? Just look at him."

It's hard to put into words what exactly Mr. Oswalt is doing. But if I had to, I'd say it's a cross between marching and catching butterflies with an imaginary net.

"Fine," I say. "But it's not like you're going to fly the plane or anything. So come on, get out."

"You don't think I know how to fly this plane?" says Hambone, giving me a look.

I look at him. He can't be serious.

"There's no way you know how to fly a plane."

"Oh, really?" says Hambone. "You didn't think I could pick a lock, and I did."

"Picking a lock and flying a plane are two totally different things."

"Is that so?"

"Yeah," I say. "I mean, you could probably teach yourself how to pick a lock. Probably saw how on YouTube. But you can't teach yourself how to fly a plane. So where did you go to learn? Snoopy's Flying Ace Academy?"

"Very funny," says Hambone. "But it's not important where I learned how."

He's right. What's important is that the zombie gorillas have found us again.

"Look, Mr. Oswalt," I say, pointing at the soccer field. "The Germans are coming. Shouldn't you get in your plane and stop them?"

Mr. Oswalt keeps marching and catching imaginary butterflies.

Boy, he really is out of it.

Now what?

Hambone turns on the engine and grabs the yoke.

"Get in," he says. "There's room."

Well, technically there is, but there isn't. Not unless I sit on his lap. Which I'm not really comfortable doing. But if it's either that or stay and get my flesh eaten off by zombie gorillas, I'm all for it.

Wait a second. I'm not getting in any plane with Hambone. What am I thinking? As if he can really fly a plane.

"Come on, Hambone," I say. "Enough fooling around. Get out of there."

Suddenly, Mr. Oswalt knocks me to the ground. "Battle stations!" he yells. "Battle stations!"

"Wait, Mr. Oswalt," I say.

He doesn't. He reaches into the cockpit, takes Hambone by the collar, and tosses him to the ground.

"Look at the pretty little lady doggies," says Hambone, obviously dazed.

I laugh. Pretty little lady doggies? That's funny.

Hambone shakes it off. "What are you laughing about? For a crazy old guy, Mr. Oswalt sure is strong," he says.

"I told you to get out of there," I say.

Mr. Oswalt jumps into the cockpit. He throws his red scarf over his shoulder and places his goggles over his eyes. He gives us the thumbs-up sign. Then he revs the engine.

I cover my ears.

Mr. Oswalt starts singing above the roar of the engine. "Off we go into the wild blue yonder, up, up, and away!"

I stand and salute Mr. Oswalt. Don't ask me why. It just feels like the right thing to do.

The plane moves forward.

I look back at the zombie gorillas. They're almost right upon us. A few more seconds, and we'll be...No. I won't even entertain the thought. It's too gruesome.

The plane picks up speed.

I look at Hambone.

He looks at me.

We both look at the plane.

"Are you thinking what I'm thinking?" I say.

He is. We run over to the plane, trying to catch up to it before it takes off into the air.

We make it.

I grab hold of one of the wires bracing the upper and lower wings. I pull myself up onto the lower wing. Hambone does the same thing on the other side.

Phew! That was close. Now all we have to do is sit and wait until we land—holding on tight to the wires, of course.

Off we go. Up, up, and away. Just like the words Mr. Oswalt is singing.

I sing along with him. So does Hambone.

All of a sudden, the plane tilts violently to one side.

I'm sliding down the wing, my arms stretching to their popping point as I desperately hold onto the wire.

The plane tilts violently to the other side.

Now I'm scrunched up against the wire, my cheek pressed into it. That's going to leave a bigger mark.

"Don't look now," says Hambone.

I look.

Oh-my-shnobbies!

I don't believe my eyes. Two zombie gorillas are sitting on either side of the plane's tail, rocking it up and down. Kind of like a teeter-totter.

How the…?

It doesn't matter. They're there—that's what matters.

And now the zombie gorilla on my side is up on its feet, getting ready to jump.

Where?

Onto the upper wing above me, it turns out. You've got to be kidding me!

The zombie gorilla swings back and forth as if it's in the jungle swinging on a tree branch.

WHAP!

It kicks me right in the kisser.

That's going to leave an even bigger mark.

WHAM!

Another kick to the face.

"Look, the little birdies are back," I say.

Come on, Peas. Snap out of it. You have to be strong.

But I'm not strong—I'm dazed.

I weeble backward.

I wobble forward.

I'm going to fall off the wing.

Before I do, I reach out, grasping for anything that might be in my reach.

Which turns out to be the zombie gorilla's dangling foot.

Gotcha!

Eww. This is one hairy zombie gorilla.

But other than that, it's not so bad. I'm feeling the wind in my face. Which is nice. And to be honest with you, I'm having a little bit of fun. Hanging on to the zombie gorilla's foot like this kind of reminds me of traveling on a zip line. Zipping through the air. What fun. I can do this all day if I have to.

Uh-oh.

I spoke too soon.

I'm slipping. Darn hairy foot.

No. It's not me. Then what is it?

Shoot.

It's the zombie gorilla. It can't hold on to the upper wing any longer. It's losing its grip.

Gradually. Gradually. Gone.

And down we go.

Down. Down. Down.

I close my eyes.

This is definitely going to leave the biggest mark yet.

CHAPTER SEVEN

As it turns out, I'm one lucky son of a gun.

I'm not going to go splat on the ground. No broken bones. Mangled limbs. Skull fractures. Not going to spend months in a hospital bed laid up in traction, spoon-fed by some nurse with a mustache and breath that smells like sardines.

No. I'm going to be just fine.

How is that possible?

For one, we were actually flying awfully low to the ground. You can't fly up, up and away when you have the added weight of me and Hambone and two zombie gorillas to deal with. In fact, we were probably lucky we didn't crash and burn.

For another, when I began my free fall, I just happened to be directly over the playground at my school.

Talk about serendipity.

I'm heading for the giant slide.

What better way to break my fall?

I reach out my arms Superman style. Look. It's a bird. It's a plane. It's me. Able to go down giant slides in a single glide.

Here we go.

I land smoothly on my stomach at the top of the slide. Whee!

When I get to the bottom, my momentum shoots me back up into the air, where I do a back summersault with a twist and land perfectly on my feet.

Totally not on purpose.

Where's somebody with a camcorder when you need one? Put it up on YouTube. I'd go viral. I'd be famous.

Oh, well.

"Everything OK there?" says Hambone, calling over to me.

"Yeah, I'm fine," I say. "Where did you come from?"

"Seriously?" he says.

"No, I mean what happened to you?" I say. "Didn't have a chance to look over. I was kind of busy dealing with my own situation."

"Yeah, I saw that," he says. "You know, you do a pretty mean imitation of a kicking dummy."

"Very funny," I say. "So what about you? Did your zombie gorilla try to kick you in the face?"

"No," he says. "I think he wanted to. But when I saw what was going on with you, I jumped for it. Did you know the sand the kindergartners have in their sandbox is surprisingly soft?"

"I did not know that," I say.

"It is," he says. "It's like fluffy pillow soft."

"Good to know," I say. "The next time I'm helplessly falling from a World War I fighter plane, I'll try to land in the sandbox."

"I recommend it."

I dust some sand out of Hambone's fur.

"I recommend never having a next time," I say. "Just think, it could have been a whole lot worse."

"Tell that to him," says Hambone.

He points to the zombie gorilla skewered on the metal tetherball pole.

"Is he...?" I say.

"I'd say so," he says. "I mean, look—the pole goes right through his eye socket."

It does. Aagh! Gross! Thanks for pointing that out to me. Love to see smashed-in zombie gorilla brains this early in the morning.

"We better get out of here before he comes back to life," I say.

Hambone gives me a look.

"What are you talking about?" he says.

"They don't stay dead, you know," I say.

"Come again?" says Hambone.

"These zombie gorillas, there is something about them," I say. "Normally you'd think you smash a zombie's brain in, that's it—it's all over. But not these guys. I'm telling you, back at the house I killed the same zombie gorilla twice."

"How do you know it was the same zombie gorilla?" he says. "It's hard to tell the difference between them."

"I know," I say. "That's why I needed to make sure. So I conducted a taste test—and both brains tasted the same to me."

"You ate zombie gorilla brains?" he says, his face contorted with revulsion.

"I needed proof," I say.

"That doesn't prove anything," he says. "Except that you've been drinking the moron juice again. Glug, glug, glug. Ahh. Hits the spot. Tasty, tasty moron juice. Makes a body strong—a big, strong moron, that is. I mean, seriously, what kind of moron does something like that? Don't you think that all zombie gorilla brains taste the same? Why would one taste different from another?" He shakes his head. "You know, if you're still hungry, I have some yellow snow you can eat. Think of it as dessert. A lemon icy."

"Make fun if you want," I say, "but I still say these zombie gorillas can come back to life. Regeneration style. Which means I don't know how we are going to stop them. Which means we'll soon be living in a world run by zombie gorillas. Shoot. I just wish I knew how it was possible for them to come back to life."

"Well," says Hambone, "when you figure that out, please let me know. But in the meantime, we have serious issues to deal with. In case you forgot, we still don't have any weapons."

I shake my head.

"What?" says Hambone. "You got something to say—spit it out."

"What good are weapons going to do if they just come back to life?" I say.

"Again with that?" he says.

"I'm just saying."

"Well what do you want to do—give up?" says Hambone. "Let those zombie gorillas eat us alive?"

"No, no," I say. "We have to do something."

"That's right," he says. "And the sooner the better. We have no idea where the other zombie gorillas are. They could be anywhere. They could be coming for us right now, for all we know."

"That's true," I say.

"I know it is," he says. "And listen, don't take this the wrong way. I know you have a keen scientific mind and everything, but what if you're wrong about those zombie gorillas? Then what? Without weapons to smash their brains in, we're goners."

"No, I hear what you're saying," I say. "And I could be wrong. I don't think I am. But even if I'm right, smashing their brains in is the only thing we have going for us right now. I mean, what are we going to do if that one on the metal tetherball pole over there suddenly comes back to life, right?"

"Right," says Hambone, rubbing his paws together. "So let's go get us some weapons so we can start doing some smashing."

He's walking over to the front entrance to the school.

"Where are you going?" I say. "It's summer—the school is closed."

"You forget about Skills and Thrills?" he says.

"Oh, yeah," I say.

Skills and Thrills is a summer school program for the behavior kids. You know, the kids who use swear words or take their clothes off in class or you-know-what on the floor in the boys' room (think the one with the two *e*'s) or throw a can of tomato soup at the teacher. (Swear. Actually happened. Kenny Martin. Second grade. Stole the can of soup from the kitchen at school. Just missed Mr. Landell's head. Bounced off the blackboard and landed at my feet.) You know, the kids who basically spend their day in the principal's office. And so if you're not in class when you should be in class, they make you go to a program over the summer called Skills and Thrills.

I get the skills part, but I'm not so sure about the thrills. What's so thrilling about summer school? Maybe they get to throw cans of tomato soup at one another. Maybe it's kind of like dodge ball. They have a bag filled with cans of tomato soup, and they stand on either side of the classroom whipping the cans at one another. That would be kind of thrilling. And potentially dangerous. Bonk! Ow, my eye!

We walk in the front entrance past the office.

The secretary doesn't even look up at us to ask what we're doing in the school. She's too busy at her computer. Which is good. There's no way I'm explaining to her that we have to look around because we need weapons to smash in the brains of these flesh-eating zombie gorillas that are on the loose thanks to Evil Doctor Crazy Gorilla unleashing them on the world so that he can take it over.

Let's just say I don't think that would go over too well.

"Hey! You're not allowed in here."

Uh-oh. Looks like I spoke too soon.

"Quick! Play dead!" I say, pushing Hambone to the ground.

He looks up at me. "What was that for?"

"Do you want to get into trouble or do you want to get weapons?"

Hambone thinks about it.

"Let me put it another way. Do you want Mrs. Wetbottom to call the cops, who will throw us in jail, where we will be sitting ducks for the zombie gorillas? Or do you want to try and pull one over on her so we can get the weapons we need to have a fighting chance?"

Hambone smirks. "Your deviousness impresses me."

"Well, we don't really have a choice. Do we?"

Hambone nods his head and winks. Then, being the pro he is lets out this very dramatic howl and rolls onto his back. Sticking his legs straight up in the air as stiff as four pieces of wood.

I want to clap my hands and yell "Bravo! Bravo!" But I don't.

Not with Mrs. Wetbottom walking right up to us.

"Young man, not only are you not allowed in school but there is absolutely, positively no dogs allowed, either."

"But can't you see he's sick," I say. "I think it's something he ate. Bad shrimp maybe."

She's not buying it. I need to think of something else. Something that would make Hambone proud.

"Please don't let anything happen to him," I say, giving her my saddest sad face. "He's my best friend in the whole world."

Mrs. Wetbottom just stares at me.

OK. OK. Looks like I better put on a show.

I drop to my knees and wrap my arms around Hambone's neck. "He's too young to die! Too young, I say! Why, it feels like just yesterday we were riding home together from the pound. I picked him because as I walked by his cage he held out his paw for me to shake. But now he'll never shake my hand again. No. He'll never again rip apart our neighbor's garbage bag to eat the dirty diapers. He'll never again chase his tail around in circles until he becomes so dizzy he falls flat on his face. He'll never again chew up a bunch of pine cones, put them in a pile, then roll on top of them to scratch his back. He'll never do anything ever again. Oh, the horror. The inhumanity."

"Is she buying it?" Hambone whispers.

I peek up at Mrs. Wetbottom.

You're not going to believe this but there are actually tears in her eyes. Slowly welling up and rolling down her cheeks.

"Oh, no," she sobs. "I will not let anything happen to your dog, young man. I could not live with myself if I did. Let me go call the nurse. Maybe she can help."

Mrs. Wetbotton goes back into the office.

"Time to amscray," I say, pulling Hambone up by the collar.

We take off and head down the front hallway, going past the library and the cafeteria.

"This way," says Hambone, turning down another hallway.

"Where are we going?" I say, following him.

"Custodian's office," he says. "That's our best bet."

Makes sense. I mean, I don't know how much time we have until Mrs. Wetbottom puts two and two together. So we need to find something fast. And our custodian is always carrying around tools. To be honest, there is a lot to fix. Our school is falling apart. Wires hang from ceiling tiles. Mold grows in the corners. The sinks don't work. Nor do the clocks or the pencil sharpeners. The floor in the boys' room smells like you-know-what. (Think the one with the two *e*'s.) It's a mess. I'm surprised the board of health hasn't condemned the place.

I follow Hambone to the custodian's office.

"Do you think he's in there?" I say.

"We're going to find out," he says.

He knocks on the door. No answer. He knocks again. Still no answer.

"Coast is clear," says Hambone.

He opens the door.

"Wow," I say. "He sure does have a lot of stuff in here." And when I say stuff, I mean man-cave stuff. Kind of like what we found in my dad's shed but different. There's an aquarium with German blue rams and black skirt tetras. A dartboard. Weights. A remote-controlled monster truck. An indoor putting green. A neon lamp.

Wow. This place has everything.

There's even a pinup calendar hanging on the wall.

"Check this out," says Hambone, taking down the calendar and flipping through the months. "It's all custodians."

He shows me July. It's a picture of a custodian hugging a mop. His lips are puckered up. As if he's going to kiss the mop head. August has a custodian wrapping himself up in duck tape. October has a custodian wearing a ballerina costume.

"Don't show me any more," I say.

"You have to see this one," says Hambone. It's December. There's a custodian dressed in a Santa suit on all fours scrubbing a toilet.

"My eyes," I say. "I'm blotting it out from my memory."

Hambone howls.

"Now I know what to get you for your birthday," he says.

He puts the pinup calendar back on the wall and goes over to the tool chest in the corner.

"There better be something good in here," he says.

There isn't.

All he finds are a hammer and a mallet.

"I guess it's better than nothing," says Hambone. "How are you with hand-to-hand combat?"

"Um, not too good," I say.

"Then we better stay close to each other," he says, handing me the hammer and keeping the mallet for himself.

The hammer feels like a toothpick in my hands. Oh, great. If a zombie gorilla has a piece of food stuck in his teeth, I'm all set.

I'm about to ask Hambone if he would like to switch weapons with me when I hear a voice behind us.

"What's going on in here?"

Chapter Eight

turn around.

Standing in the doorway with his hands on his hips is Mr. O'Dongle. Our custodian. Are you kidding me? Could it be any harder to sneak into school and get weapons? Wow. I'm starting to think it might not be worth the effort.

"You have about three seconds to tell me what you think you're doing in my office," says Mr. O'Dongle. "And it better be the truth."

I look over at Hambone. He nods his approval.

"We need weapons," I say.

"Weapons?" says Mr. O'Dongle. "What do you need weapons for?"

I look over at Hambone again. He nods again.

Boy, how am I going to put this? If saying that Hambone is a dog that can walk and talk just like a kid will get me sent to the loony bin, then where will I get sent if I tell Mr. O'Dongle that there are flesh-eating zombie gorillas trying to take over the world?

Here goes nothing.

"Well, you see, we need weapons to kill the...um... well, you're not going to believe this but there are these gorillas...well, they're not really gorillas technically they are kind of sort of like...well, they're kind of like...um, like zombies."

"Zombies? Did you say zombies?" says Mr. O'Dongle, clasping his hands together and jumping up and down as if he's on a pogo stick. "Oh, goody, goody!"

I give Hambone a look. He shrugs his shoulders. Yeah, I agree, definitely not the reaction I was expecting. Can you say totally wacko?

Mr. O'Dongle starts pacing back and forth. "Ok. Calm down. Get your body under control. Deep breath. In. Out. Good. Now, what's the first thing we need to do? The first thing we need to do is get our supplies ready."

"Supplies?" I say. "Supplies for what?"

"Why, to survive the zombie attack, of course." Mr. O'Dongle goes over to a locked cabinet attached to the wall. "Thank goodness I'm prepared. Warm blankets, water, freeze-dried food, first-aid kit, a solar charger, radar backpack, satellite radio. They are all in here." He opens the cabinet. "See?"

"I've been preparing for this day my entire life," he continues. "Those zombies aren't going to get me. No way. No how. I bet they're going to get that sales clerk. I bet he regrets giving me a funny look. I bet he wishes he has what I have. Too bad. Survival of the fittest." He grabs a five-gallon bottle of water. "How many of these do you think you can carry?"

"Um, I don't know," I say.

"Better pack as many as we can," he says, grabbing a giant duffle bag from the top shelf. Then he sings as he packs the supplies. "I've got zombies on a zombie day. I bet you say what can make me feel this way? Zombies. Zombies. Talking about zombies."

As Mr. O'Dongle continues to sing and pack, I tiptoe over to Hambone.

"Does he expect us to go with him?"

"I don't know," whispers Hambone. "But I do know that we don't have time for this. We have to get out of here."

Hambone is right. Luckily, Mr. O'Dongle isn't paying any attention to us. He's too busy singing and packing.

"Let's sneak out of here," I say.

"Wait a second," says Hambone, grabbing a can of spray paint on his way out of the custodian's office. "We're going to need this, too."

"What's that for?" I say.

"I've been thinking," says Hambone. "We kind of need to know if you're right about that whole zombie-gorilla-coming-back-to-life thing. If you're right, we're in trouble. So I figure after we smash their brains in, we can spray a mark or something on their fur. Like a tag. And if we see any of those with that tag again, we'll know."

"So you believe me," I say, putting my hands over my heart. "I'm touched. Deeply, deeply touched."

"You sure are," he says, smirking. "A little touched in the head, that is."

I look down both ends of the hallway. "Which way?"

Suddenly, there's a commotion. Loud voices. Footsteps. Somebody screams. A door slams.

"What do you think is going on?" I say.

"Only one way to find out," says Hambone.

He starts down the hallway.

"Wait," I say. But it's too late. He's already gone.

I take a deep breath and follow close behind.

"I think it's coming from one of the fourth-grade classrooms," I say. "Maybe even my old room."

The commotion gets louder.

"This way," says Hambone. "And remember to stay close. If it's who I think it is, we'll be better off working together."

I don't want it to be who he thinks it is.

I want it to be cute little pink fluffy bunny rabbits hopping around all nice and happy like. Hippity-hop. Hippity-hop. Isn't the world a wonderful pace?

But I know it isn't.

CRASH!

Something flies through the window in front of us, shattering the glass and landing by our feet.

It's a can of tomato soup.

I look in the classroom where it came from.

GULP!

Zombie gorillas! And they've got the behavior kids backed up in a corner!

Some of the behavior kids are standing up on the desks, kicking at the zombie gorillas to keep them away. Kenny Martin is one of them. Except he keeps reaching into a bag he has with him on the desk and taking out cans of tomato soup to throw at the zombie gorillas. (I was just kidding about the bag full of tomato soup cans, by the way. I didn't think that was a real thing. But maybe I'm psychic—you know, have that ESP stuff. That would be cool.)

The zombie gorillas get closer and closer. It doesn't look as if the behavior kids will be able to hold them off much longer.

Oh-my-shneggies!

I've never seen somebody get their flesh eaten off before. And I don't think I want to now.

One of the zombie gorillas grabs Kenny Martin by the neck. Kenny tries hitting it on the head with a can of tomato soup. That doesn't work. The zombie gorilla just grunts. Kenny struggles. As he's struggling, he makes eye contact with me. He mouths something. I think he's saying, "Help me!"

Should I? I don't know. I'm kind of in a quandary here.

Now, before you say that I have to help Kenny because human beings have an obligation to help other human beings who are in trouble, and before you say that if I don't help him, I'm a horrible human being—which I'm not; I'm a nice human being—let me just say that I haven't mentioned everything there is to mention about Kenny Martin. Like he's the biggest bully in the school and makes my life a living H-E-double-hockey-sticks on a daily basis. Why I failed to mention this is probably because it's not my favorite thing to talk about. Obviously.

I think about what I should do.

Is it really a bad thing if the zombie gorilla eats Kenny's flesh off? I mean, I have thought of worse things I would like to do to him. Like this medieval punishment I read about. You tie the person's arms and legs down, and then you cover their stomach with a metal cage with a rat inside. The cage is heated until the rat starts ripping out the person's intestines and other internal organs to escape. Now wouldn't that be worse for Kenny?

So you see, I'm really trying to look on the bright side of things. That's how nice I am.

OK. You're right. That's silly. I know. And I hope you know that I would never subject Kenny to any kind of medieval punishment. It's just the victim in me talking.

Speaking of victims, Kenny's eyes are starting to bulge out.

I have to do something. Quick.

I throw my hammer as hard as I can at the zombie gorilla. It hits it in the back. The zombie gorilla drops Kenny and turns around. It grunts at me.

"How'd that work out for you?" says Hambone.

It didn't. Not only did I lose my weapon, but the only thing I accomplished was making the zombie gorilla angry. In fact, I made all of the zombie gorillas angry. Because they all turn around.

"Ah, we better get out of here," I say.

"Right behind you, buddy," says Hambone.

We take off.

The zombie gorillas chase after us.

Here we go again. But at least they're leaving the behavior kids alone now. That's a good thing. So if these zombie gorillas catch up to us and eat our flesh off, at least I can say the last thing I did before I turned into a zombie gorilla was save a bunch of kids who like to swear in class. Now am I such a horrible human being?

At the end of the hallway, we burst through the door and out onto the playground. Hambone stops and goes back over to the door. He secures his mallet in between the handles so the zombie gorillas can't open it from their side.

Then we run, run, run.

Chapter Nine

"I'm sick of all this running," says Hambone. He stops by the side of the road and puts his hands on his knees. He's panting like mad.

"You're just out of shape," I say.

"Being out of shape has nothing to do with it," he says. "What's the point of all this running? It's not doing anything for us. It's not like I'm training for the Olympics."

"Let's just take a breather," I say. I put my arms up over my head. It's something our gym teacher, Mr. Rigstein, tells us to do when we're tired from running. "Once we catch our breath, then we can figure out what to do next."

"That's what I'm talking about," says Hambone, standing up straight. "What are we doing? Are we going to run away every time we face these zombie gorillas, or are we going to stand our ground and smash their brains in?"

"Hey, I didn't force you to run away," I say. "You came willingly, remember? If you wanted, you could have stayed there and gone all Bruce Lee-like with your mallet. Which, by the way, I don't think would have been such a good idea."

"Point taken," he says. "But don't you agree that this is a waste?"

"What do you mean?" I say.

"Hold on a second," he says. "I have to see a man about a dog."

Hambone goes over to a fire hydrant and lifts his leg up.

I look away. No need to see that, if you know what I'm saying. It's bad enough I can hear the psss sound. (Think the one with two *e*'s.)

"So let me tell you what I mean," he says, doing his business. "What did running away do for us? We lost our weapons again, so we need to find new ones. Again. And we didn't even have a chance to tag any of the zombie gorillas with the spray paint. So we're back to where we started. It's frustrating is all I'm saying."

"I agree," I say. "But we have to be careful. That definitely wasn't the time or the place to fight the zombie gorillas. We're lucky we got out alive."

Hambone finishes up. "When exactly will be the time and place?" he says, shaking his leg. "Before we know it, there won't be any more times or places. Zoo—no. Backyard—no. School—no. It's getting ridiculous."

"Not as ridiculous as having our flesh eaten off by zombie gorillas trying to take over the world," I say.

"Why do you keep saying that?" says Hambone, walking back over to me. "I mean, how do you know they're trying to take over the world?"

"It's the only thing that makes sense," I say. "I mean, what else are they doing? And why did Evil Doctor Crazy Gorilla turn the gorillas into zombies in the first place? He has to have a reason. Just like Principal Mallory tells us at every single assembly: there is a reason for everything we do. Either it's a good reason or a bad reason. But there is a reason. If you don't have a reason for doing something, you're not thinking hard enough. Well, Evil Doctor Crazy Gorilla is thinking. Plenty hard. He's thinking that he wants to take over the world. And he's using zombie gorillas to do just that."

"You're probably right," says Hambone. "But that just proves my point. We have to stop running away before it's too late."

"I know, I know," I say.

Just then, I hear a buzzing sound in the distance. Oh, no. That's all we need. Killer bees. Could this day get much worse? But as I keep listening, I notice the buzzing sound changing. It goes from buzzing to growling. That's not killer bees. That's zombie gorillas!

I step into the street to see where they're coming from.

"If this is who I think it is, you know what to do, right?" I say.

"What's that?" says Hambone.

"Run," I say.

Hambone looks at me, frowning.

"Not the time or place again?" he says.

"Do we have any weapons?" I say. "I didn't think so. But if you want to stay, be my guest. Have fun. It was nice knowing you."

"Oh, don't be like that," he says, coming over to me and putting his arm around my shoulder. "You'll miss me if I'm gone."

"Don't think so," I say, shrugging him off. "I'll just go to the pound again and get a new dog."

"I'm just busting your chops," he says. "Why are you getting so mad?"

"Because this is serious," I say. "The fate of the world is on our hands. So stop fooling around and be serious."

"OK, OK," he says. He crosses his arms over his chest, purses his lips, and narrows his eyes.

"What are you doing?" I say.

"This is me being serious," he says.

It doesn't last. Right after he says that, he breaks down laughing.

So much for being serious. I guess you really can't teach an old dog new tricks.

Oh, well. I don't have time to worry about that.

The growling is getting closer.

I bend down and touch my toes. Got to stretch. Don't want to pull a hammy at a time like this.

"Can you see them yet?" says Hambone.

"Just about," I say. "They're coming around the corner now."

I get myself ready in a good runner's position.

On your mark. Get set.

There they are!

Wait a second.

Those aren't zombie gorillas. It's just a bunch of big, dirty, hairy guys on Harleys. So that was the growling sound—their motorcycles. Phew! I can't tell you how happy I am to see a motorcycle gang. In fact, I don't think I've been happier in all my life.

The lead motorcycle guy stops in front of me and Hambone. He straddles his Harley. It's sparkly pink and purple. Interesting choice of colors. I bet he must be the leader of the gang. He's bigger and dirtier and hairier than the others. He's wearing an American-flag bandana on his head, thick goggles, and a black leather jacket. He also has a goatee and a scar that goes from his right eye across to his right ear. On his left forearm, he's got a tattoo of a German soldier with an X through it. The tattoo looks like he drew it on with a ball-point pen.

"Hey, kid," he says to me. "You seen any of those Germans around here?"

"Excuse me?" I say.

"Germans?" he says. "Don't you know we're under attack by the Germans? It's like Pearl Harbor all over again."

"I think he's been drinking too much motor oil, if you know what I mean," whispers Hambone.

"Shh," I say. "Stay back and let me handle this."

"What's a matter, kid?" says the leader. "Can't you talk? Are they watching? Is that it?" He looks around suspiciously. "Do they have a sniper up there in that tree? Is that it? Did they tell you to get rid of us, and if you don't, they'll shoot your dog? Those cowards. Shooting a kid's dog." He looks around again. "I know it's not safe to talk, but if what I'm saying is true, blink your eyes once."

"I'm sorry, sir," I say. "But it doesn't make any sense. Who said there were Germans around here?"

"That's what some crazy old guy said right after he landed his plane practically on top of us," says the leader. "Got out and started screaming that the Germans were coming."

Oh. Now it makes sense.

"That was Mr. Oswalt," I say. "He thinks they're Germans, but they're really zombie gorillas."

"Come again, kid?" says the leader.

"Zombie gorillas," I repeat. "We're being attacked by zombie gorillas."

"Zombie gorillas, you say? Huh?" says the leader. He turns to the rest of his motorcycle gang. "Did you hear that, boys? Now we're after zombie gorillas. What do you think about that?"

The other motorcycle guys cheer, whooping and hollering at the top of their lungs.

"See?" says the leader. "It's all the same to us. But first, I have to do this." He takes a ball-point pen and draws a zombie gorilla on his right forearm. It's really good. Surprisingly accurate.

He admires his handiwork a moment, and then he puts an X through it.

"Now we're ready," he says.

"Ready for what?" I say.

"To get us some of these zombie gorillas," says the leader.

Looks like he's about to get his wish. Here come the zombie gorillas knuckle-walking down the street. And they're not getting the funniest looks from everyone they meet. In fact, there's nobody on the street. And even if there were, nobody would think it funny to see zombie gorillas coming.

I know I sure don't.

"Excuse me, sir," I say. "But those zombie gorillas you want are right behind you."

"Hey, thanks, kid," says the leader. "You are now about to witness the strength of the Mama's Boys—the biggest, baddest motorcycle gang on the planet."

He points to the insignia on the back of his leather jacket. It's a lady's head with the words "I heart Mama" above it. Then he signals for the rest of his gang to turn their motorcycles around and go after the zombie gorillas.

They do.

"Let's get out of here quick," I say, going over to Hambone. "Before it gets ugly."

"No way," he says. "I want to see what happens. Mama's Boys versus zombie gorillas. Are you kidding? You can't make this stuff up."

"Do I have to drag you out of here by the collar?" I say.

"You couldn't if you tried," he says. "Besides, this is a golden opportunity for us."

"What do you mean?" I say.

"Aren't you forgetting about this?" he says, showing me the can of spray paint. "All we have to do is wait for one of the zombie gorillas to get his brains smashed in by one of the Mama's Boys, and then we can tag it. You see what I'm saying? This way we can find out once and for all if they come back to life. Which is kind of important, right?"

Darn him. He's right. We have to do this. But if we do it, we're going to do it from a safe distance.

I tell this to Hambone.

"But we can't be so far away we can't see what's going on," he says. "What good will that do?"

I point to a row of hedges a few feet back from the street. The good thing about them is that they're close enough to the action but also bushy enough that if things get hairy, we can duck behind them for cover.

It's a perfect compromise. So we go over and settle into our spots.

"By the way," says Hambone. "How stupid is the name Mama's Boys?"

"Pretty stupid," I say. "Definitely doesn't instill fear when you hear it."

"I have a perfect one for your gang," he says.

"Oh, yeah?" I say. "What is it?"

"Sir Peas-A-Lot and His Merry Band of Green Veggies."

"Very funny," I say. "I like the pun. And that way nobody would think the one with the two *e*'s, right?"

"Exactly," says Hambone. "See, I'm just looking out for you."

"Gee, thanks," I say. "OK. Your turn now. What would you call your motorcycle gang if you had one?"

Hambone thinks. "The Mongrels," he says.

That is awesome. But I'm not going to tell him that. I won't give him the satisfaction.

Petty? Yes. But he deserves it after the name he gave my gang.

Speaking of gangs, the leader of the Mama's Boys stops his motorcycle in front of the zombie gorillas. He stares them down. Then he takes his pointer finger and drags it across his throat. The zombie gorillas just grunt. Symbolic gestures are lost on them.

Oh, well.

It's go time.

On the leader's signal, the Mama's Boys attack the zombie gorillas. Some crash their motorcycles right into them, while others jump off and bull rush the zombie gorillas, wielding foam swords, rubber bands, jump ropes, and squirt guns.

"You've got to be kidding me," I say. "Are these guys for real?"

"Obviously, they've never been in a fight before," says Hambone. "In fact, I don't think these guys could fight their way out of a wet paper bag. Five bucks says this is over in two minutes."

"I hope you're wrong," I say. "I want to tag one of these zombie gorillas as soon as possible."

Hambone howls. "Seriously? You think any of these guys are going to kill a zombie gorilla? With the weapons they brought? You have a better chance of being a kid that can walk and bark and do everything any dog can do as long as no one else is around."

"Maybe we could make some better weapons."

"Out of what? Just sit back and enjoy the show."

But what happens next I wouldn't exactly call a show. More like a beat down.

"Ouch, that's got to hurt," I say as a zombie gorilla snatches a squirt gun out of the hands of one of the Mama's Boys and proceeds to repeatedly whack him over the head with it. Over and over until he collapses to the ground in a heap of leather.

Another one pinned underneath his motorcycle acts as a trampoline for two baby zombie gorillas.

"This is getting ugly," says Hambone.

And it is.

Everywhere I look, the zombie gorillas are pummeling the Mama's Boys. They're falling down all over the street. Some are trying desperately to get back on their motorcycles.

No luck.

Zombie gorillas stop them and then proceed to tear into their flesh.

Oh, the screams. I cover my ears. But I should really cover my eyes. Don't want to see the giant chunks of flesh being ripped off. No. There's too much blood. There's too much carnage.

"This is horrible," I say. "There goes tagging one of the zombie gorillas. Now what?"

Miraculously, the leader of the Mama's Boys is still alive. He picks up a jump rope and swings it over his head, gathering momentum for what he does with it next: fling it at the zombie gorilla lunging for him.

"Gotcha," says the leader as the jump rope wraps several times around the zombie gorilla's neck.

He yanks down hard on the jump rope, forcing the zombie gorilla to the ground. Then he spins the zombie gorilla around like a hammer thrower in a track-and-field event. Once the zombie gorilla is elevated high enough off the ground, he releases his grip, sending the zombie gorilla sailing through the air.

It lands by us, head splattering open like an overripe cantaloupe.

"Please resist the urge to eat some," says Hambone.

"Very funny," I say. "Now tag him—quick."

Hambone does.

"A smiley face?" I say.

"Why not?" says Hambone.

The leader of the Mama's Boys runs over to us. "Hey, kid, what are you doing here? Can't you see this is no place for you and your dog? Now go."

"I would love to, sir," I say. "But unfortunately we have to stick around a little while longer."

"Oh, yeah?" says the leader. "Why's that?"

I tell him.

"Are you pulling my leg, kid?" he says.

"No, sir," I say. "Swear."

"OK," he says. "If you say so."

But I don't think he really believes me. Because he gives me a look and then pokes at the zombie gorilla with the toe of his boot.

"Seems plenty dead to me, and that's the way he's gonna stay," says the leader.

"I hope I'm wrong," I say.

The leader gives me another look.

"OK," he says. "How 'bout I keep checking in on you just in case?"

"That would be awesome," I say. "Thanks."

He goes off and fights more zombie gorillas.

Me and Hambone duck back to our spots behind the hedges and watch.

"Look at that one," I say as a zombie gorilla is tossed high into the air. "Look like anyone you know?"

Hambone growls.

"Aw, come on," I say. "That was funny. I mean, a zombie gorilla did the exact same thing to you. Of course, I think you were more airborne. On account of you being lighter."

He growls some more.

"What's the matter?" I say. "You can bust everybody else's chops, but the second somebody does it to you, you get all mad? That's a little unfair, don't you think?"

More growling.

"Oh, I'm so scared," I say. "But you can stop now—I get the point."

But Hambone doesn't stop.

OK. He's going too far now. And I'm going to tell him so.

I look at Hambone.

OH-MY-SHNOOKIES!

That wasn't Hambone growling. That was the zombie gorilla.

The previously-dead-and-tagged-with-a-smiley-face-but-now-back-to-life zombie gorilla.

And he's got Hambone by the throat.

I pick up the can of spray paint by the zombie gorilla's foot. Hambone must have dropped it when he got grabbed.

I spray the zombie gorilla in the eyes. It's the only thing I can think of doing. It doesn't help. In fact, I think it just makes the zombie gorilla squeeze Hambone's neck harder. More veins are popping out.

What am I going to do now?

"Stand back," says a voice. It's the leader of the Mama's Boys. He's going to help Hambone. And not a moment too soon.

He jumps on the zombie gorilla's back and yells, "Leave him alone you big bully."

The zombie gorilla staggers backwards, still holding onto Hambone. So the leader thumps it on the head. "I said leave him alone."

This aggravates the zombie gorilla. I think. I don't know. All I know is that it lets go of Hambone and then throws the leader to the ground.

"OK," says the leader, getting up on his feet. "Now get out of here while you still can."

He doesn't have to tell us twice. We hightail it out of there faster than you can say "Kenny Martin is a mama's boy."

CHAPTER TEN

T his isn't good.
This isn't good.
This isn't good.
No. It's terrible.
This is terrible.
This is terrible.
This is terrible.

"What are you babbling about over there?" says Hambone.

"Oh, nothing," I say. "It's only my worst fear has now been realized, that's all."

(Up until this point, my worst fears have been [1] being trapped in a coffin filled with spiders, [2] being trapped in a bathtub filled with poisonous snakes, [3] being shrunk to miniature size and then running from a giant crack opening up in the earth only to fall through that crack, turning everything pitch black and covering me with slime so I can't breathe, and [4] taking a shower and closing my eyes and suddenly being covered with snakes crawling into my mouth and spitting out white fuzz. But now, right up there at numero uno is zombie gorillas that won't die. Worst fear ever!)

I look around.

It's probably all this talk about worst fears, but it seems that behind every tree, zombie gorillas are lurking. Licking their chops. Salivating over the prospect of more flesh. My flesh. And there's nothing I can do to stop them.

Boy, the woods seemed like the perfect place to hide out when Hambone suggested it, but now I'm regretting the move.

"Are you OK?" says Hambone, jumping down off the rock he's been sitting on and coming over to me. "Looks like you're about to you-know-what yourself."

I'm not. I'm afraid. But not that afraid. Well...OK... yes, I'm that afraid. You got me. If I'm not careful, a little leakage may happen. Well...OK...a lot of leakage may happen. Like Niagara Falls down the front of my pants.

"What are we going to do now?" I say. "We better think of something fast."

"I'm open to any ideas you have," says Hambone.

The trouble is I don't have any. I need to think. Think. Think. Think.

"What do you think happened to the Mama's Boys?" I say. Totally off topic. But it was something I was thinking.

"You ever hear of being in a turkey coma because you've eaten too much turkey on Thanksgiving?" says Hambone. "Well, I bet those zombie gorillas are in a Mama's Boys coma right about now." He pretends to fall asleep and then wakes up suddenly and burps. "Mmm, that sure was some good Mama's Boys. Tasted like chicken."

"Yeah, I guess you're right," I say, a little dejected. "I was kind of hoping that wasn't the case. I liked the Mama's Boys."

"Not as much as those zombie gorillas did," says Hambone, rubbing his belly.

"Don't make fun," I say. "How easily you forget that the leader helped you out. Saved you from getting squeezed to death. You should probably feel a little bad that he most likely got eaten, don't you think?"

"Hey," says Hambone, "I'm eternally grateful to him. Don't get me wrong. But he's a zombie gorilla now. And there's nothing we can do about that. But hey, maybe you wish it was you. It could have been the other way around very easily, you know."

"I don't want to think about that," I say.

"Good," says Hambone. "Because we need you to think about how we're going to stop these zombie gorillas."

"Me?" I say. "Why can't you come up with anything?"

"You're the expert when it comes to horror movies, remember?" he says. "Just think back to all the ones you've seen. There must be something in one of them that can help."

"That's the problem," I say. "In none of the horror movies I've seen have the zombie gorillas come back to life. Once you smash their brains in, they're dead. And they stay dead. This is completely different. It's terrible."

"There has to be something," says Hambone, pacing back and forth. "I'll keep smashing their brains in if I have to. But I'd rather not have to, if you know what I mean."

"I hear what you're saying. But I don't know. I wish I could go up to Evil Doctor Crazy Gorilla and ask him how he did it."

Wait a second.

"That's it," I say.

"What's it?" says Hambone.

"Evil Doctor Crazy Gorilla," I say. "He's a crazy mad-scientist guy. And it was his green potion that turned the ordinary gorillas into zombie gorillas."

"Yeah, so?" says Hambone.

"So. In all the movies with mad scientists I've seen, they don't just make potions. They also make antidotes. Just in case something goes terribly wrong."

Hambone clasps his paws together. "Perfect," he says. "And if we have the antidote, we can turn the zombie gorillas back into ordinary gorillas, right?"

"That's how we'll stop them," I say. "Of course, the only question now is how do we find Evil Doctor Crazy Gorilla so we can get our hands on that antidote?"

Hambone grins from ear to ear.

"I have an idea," he says.

"Great," I say. "What is it?"

"You're going to love it."

Uh-oh. The last time Hambone said I was going to love one of his ideas was the time he wanted me to play dead on the train tracks. What a spectacularly bad idea that turned out to be. Let me tell you about it. Hambone said it would be funny. He said I should jump up once the train stopped and yell, "Boogie, boogie." He said the look on the engineer's face would be priceless. I said what if he doesn't stop. Hambone said he can get thrown in jail if he doesn't, so he has to stop. Well, let me tell you he doesn't have to stop. Especially if he doesn't see you because the sun reflecting off the metal tracks bores into his eyes, blinding him. I'm just lucky I have really good reflexes. I'd have gotten flattened flatter than a pancake. Of course, Hambone thought my near brush with death was the funniest thing he'd ever seen. He was laughing so hard he almost went into cardiac arrest.

"Are you ready to hear my idea?" says Hambone, nodding his head.

I brace myself. "Can't wait."

"OK," he says. "You know how I spent all that time in the pound on Kenny Lane?"

"Yeah." That's where I got Hambone. Not the nicest place in the world. You walked in and—bam! Doggie odor. And not the good kind. If there is a good kind.

"And you know the security guard there?" he continues. "The one who sat on his butt all night long when he should have been walking around?"

"Didn't he just watch movies or something?" I say.

"That's the one."

"What about him?"

"Nothing," says Hambone, frowning. "I'd like to forget everything about him. But what I can't forget about is the movie he watched every single night."

"Let me guess," I say. "It was *King Kong*."

Hambone eyes me suspiciously. "Have I told you this before?"

"Not exactly," I say. "I just put it together right now, if you want to know the truth. I knew something happened to you with that movie when you were younger. That's why you hate gorillas, right?"

"Yeah, well, let me tell you," he says, "watching that movie ad nauseam would make anyone a gorilla hater. But that's not the point. The point is the movie holds the key to us finding Evil Doctor Crazy Gorilla."

"How is that possible?" I say, shrugging.

Hambone gives me a knowing look. "The key rhymes with shady."

"Come again?" I say.

As you've probably already realized, Hambone isn't shy about saying what's on his mind. Typically not filtering any of it. So I'm not sure why he's all of a sudden speaking in riddles now.

But I'm sure I'm going to find out.

"What rhymes with shady?" says Hambone.

"I don't know," I say. "I'm not good at rhyming."

"Come on, think," prods Hambone. "Frady? Spady? Zady?"

"Drawing a blank here."

Hambone throws his paws up in disgust. "It's lady. Lady. Lady. Lady."

"OK."

I still have no idea where this is going.

"What does this have to do with the movie?" I say.

"I'm getting there," says Hambone. "In the movie, there's this lady. Ann. Kong likes Ann. He goes gaga over her and doesn't want anything bad to happen to her, so he takes her to his cave to protect her. Comprende?"

I nod. "Lady. Ann. Kong. Gaga. Cave. Got it."

"Good," says Hambone. "Now gorillas and zombie gorillas are basically the same thing. Same DNA. Which means if a zombie gorilla sees someone that looks like Ann, it's going to want to take her someplace safe where nothing bad can happen to her."

"I guess," I say. "Keep going."

Hambone stares at me. "That's it. That's my idea for finding Evil Doctor Crazy Gorilla."

"I'm sorry," I say. "I must have missed something. What's your idea again?"

"You should dress up like Ann."

I'm stunned. I'm mortified. Bowled over. At a loss. "Me? You want me to dress up like Ann? The lady in the movie?"

"That's right."

"Oh, no."

"Oh, yes."

This can't be happening. Just when you think it can't get any worse than playing dead on the train tracks—now comes this spectacularly bad idea: dressing up like a lady.

"Why don't you do it?" I say. "It's your idea."

"I would, but a zombie gorilla will never buy it," says Hambone. "Me, a lady? Look at my legs—they're all hairy."

I shake my head. "What zombie gorilla would think I was a lady?"

"Are you kidding?" says Hambone, smiling. "Put one of your mother's dresses on you, some jewelry, maybe a little makeup, some rouge, and voila: what zombie gorilla wouldn't think you were a lady?"

I shake my head some more. "You're crazy if you think I'm going to dress up like a lady."

"You have to," says Hambone. "It's the only way we'll ever find Evil Doctor Crazy Gorilla."

"How is my dressing up like a lady going to help us find Evil Doctor Crazy Gorilla?"

Hambone rolls his eyes. "Have you not been listening to a single word I've said? OK. I'll walk you through it again. You dress up like Ann. The zombie gorilla goes gaga over you. He grabs you. He takes you someplace safe."

"I got that part," I say. "But where does Evil Doctor Crazy Gorilla come in?"

"I guarantee you he'll be in the same place where the zombie gorilla takes you," says Hambone.

"And if he isn't there?"

"He will be."

"And if he isn't?"

"You got any other ideas?"

I don't. But I'm thinking. I'm thinking how if I don't think of something else fast, this is what we have to go with.

Hambone walks over to me and puts his arm around my shoulder. "I know you have some misgivings about this. Believe me, if I had any other ideas that I thought would work, I'd tell you. But I don't. This is the one. It'll work. It's foolproof. And just think: you do this, and we end up turning those zombie gorillas back into ordinary gorillas. How awesome will that be, right?"

"Pretty awesome," I say.

"That's right," says Hambone, patting me on the chest. "And what's more, just think about what will happen after: we'll be famous. They'll dedicate statues made in our likeness. We'll be known forever as Peas and Hambone: the kids who rid the world of zombie gorillas. Saved the human race. Let freedom ring."

I think I've heard this before.

"And all because of you, Peas, my man," he continues. "All because you had the courage—no, the fortitude—to put aside your doubts and fears and do this." His face softens. "I'm in awe of you, Peas. I really am." He starts bowing in front of me. "I bow down to your superior guts. Bow. Bow."

I know he's just messing with me. Trying to persuade me to dress up like a lady. But it works. "Get up," I say.

"So you'll do it?"

Of course I will. The fate of the world depends upon it.

CHAPTER ELEVEN

'm standing in front of a full-length mirror wearing nothing but my underwear and a bra.

"Here. Try this one," says Hambone, handing me another one of my mother's dresses. The first hundred or so he had me try on were either too long or too short, so I'm hoping this one is just right.

I take the dress off the hanger.

Boy, am I glad nobody's home. How embarrassing that would be if they walked in on me right now. You know, when my parents said they were taking my older brother back-to-school shopping today without me, I was a little mad. But now I couldn't be happier they are doing that.

I hand the hanger to Hambone and put on the dress.

"So?" says Hambone, grinning. "What do you think?"

"I think you're enjoying this way too much," I say.

"That's beside the point," he says. "So, have we found the one you just absolutely have to have? Is it to die for?" He giggles and puts his paw up to his mouth. "Oops. Bad choice of words."

"You know," I say, tugging my bra back up to my chest. Again. It keeps slipping because it's too big. "This may come as a big shock to you, but making fun like you are isn't helping."

"Aw, come on," he says. "If I can't have some fun with this, what can I have fun with? I mean, it's not every day my best friend dresses up like a lady. You want me to give up a golden opportunity like this?"

I guess not. "Just keep the jokes to a minimum. OK?"

Hambone makes an X over his heart. "Swear," he says. Then out of the corner of his mouth, he adds, "You're lucky I'm not taking pictures."

"Hey."

"Just kidding."

He'd better be.

I look at myself in the full-length mirror.

This dress definitely fits the best. Wait a second. I mean, it's not like I know how a dress is supposed to fit. Don't get the wrong idea. I've never worn a dress before. I mean, well, yes, maybe, one time I did wear a dress, but it was part of a Halloween costume—I was a wizard. Plus, I was like six or something.

"Turn around," says Hambone, twirling his finger at me. "Let me get a good look at you."

"Seriously?" I say.

"Just do it."

I turn around.

"Wait a second," says Hambone. He walks behind me and tucks in the tag in the back. "There."

"All better now?" I say.

"You can't have a tag showing. That's not very lady-like," he says. He steps to the side and looks at me in the full-length mirror. "So?"

I shrug. "It's good enough, I guess."

"Good enough?" he says. "Do you know what I'm looking at?"

No. And I can't wait to hear.

"I'm looking at the spitting image of Ann," he continues. "Wow. If I didn't know any better, I'd say you were her."

"Very funny," I say.

"No, I'm serious," he says. (Yeah, right.) "There's not one zombie gorilla that's going to know the difference. I mean there's no way one of them is going to stop and say, 'Hey, this isn't a lady. This is Peas in a dress.'" He stops and flashes me a mischievous smile. "Hey, that wasn't half bad. Get it. Peas in a dress? Psss!"

He breaks down laughing.

"Oh, so this is funny, huh?" I say. "Funny? I'll show you funny. I'll take this thing off right now. See how it fits you." I threaten to unzip the dress. "Better start shaving your legs."

Hambone gathers himself together. "Now, now," he says. "I'll give it to you—that last part might have been a little too much. But all joking aside, let's not forget what we're doing this for. The human race is counting on you."

"Fine," I say. "Let's just go before I change my mind."

I start putting on my high heels.

"Wait, wait," says Hambone. "Before we go we need some final touches."

He goes into my mother's dresser and takes out a silver necklace and silver clip-on earrings. He hands them to me.

"Do I have to?" I say.

"Gorillas like silvery things," he says.

I put them on.

Hambone goes into my mother's makeup case and takes out a tube of lipstick.

"Pucker up," he says.

"Do I have to?" I say.

"Human race," he says. "Remember the human race."

I pucker up.

Boy, this better work. If I do all this and the zombie gorilla just eats my flesh off? What a way to go. And just think, my last memories will be of me standing in my mother's bedroom getting dressed up like a lady. Lipstick and all.

Hambone looks me over. "OK," he says. "I think we're good to go." He steps aside. "After you."

I take a deep breath.

You can do this, I say to myself. You can do this.

But what I can't do is walk in high heels.

It goes something like this: Click. Click. Swud!

The clicks are the sound the high heels make hitting the hardwood floor in my mother's bedroom. The swud is the sound I make hitting the hardwood floor in my mother's bedroom.

Ouch!

I rub my butt. If this keeps up, my butt is going to be one giant black-and-blue mark.

I get up.

I steady myself.

"Maybe go slower this time," offers Hambone.

"You think?"

Just then, Hambone lets one rip.

"Hey," I say. "I'm trying to walk here. The least you can do is say excuse me."

"Why?"

"Um, you just farted."

"No I didn't."

"You sure did. I heard it."

"It wasn't me. Must have been somebody else."

I turn back around and give him a look. "We're the only ones here."

"It wasn't me," he says, shooing me forward.

Whatever.

Click. Click. Click. Click.

"Atta boy," says Hambone. "Now you're getting the hang of it."

And I am. I get all the way down the stairs and into the living room without falling once. Not too bad if I do say so myself.

I pause at the front door.

"Well, what are you waiting for?" says Hambone impatiently.

"Just give me a second," I say.

I take another deep breath.

You can do this, I say to myself again. You can do this. Yes, the world's fate rests on your shoulders. Yes, we don't have much time. Don't think about that. Don't think about how far the zombie gorillas have gotten—how many people they have eaten and turned into more zombie gorillas. Wait a second. Do you think they got to the mall where my family is? Are they now zombie gorillas? For all you know, it could already be too late. You don't stand a chance. No. You can't think about that. You have to think positively. There's still time. You can still get to Evil Doctor Crazy Gorilla and find the antidote that will turn these zombie gorillas back into ordinary gorillas. All you have to do is be the best lady you can be.

Speaking of being the best, Hambone lets another one rip.

"Again?" I say.

"What?" he says.

"Come on," I say. "Are you going to tell me that wasn't you as well? It sounded like it started rumbling around in your stomach, picked up steam in your intestines, and then growled its way out your butt."

"It wasn't me," he says.

"It's OK to admit you have serious gas issues," I say, turning around to look at him.

OH-MY-SNEGGIES!

Hambone was telling the truth. It wasn't him. The sounds I heard were coming from zombie gorillas. They're in the house!

"Quick!" I yell. "Run!"

"What?" says Hambone, not moving. He doesn't see the zombie gorillas knuckle-walking down the hallway toward him.

I grab Hambone by the collar. "We have to get to the basement," I say, dragging him with me.

Click-click-click-click-click-click-slam!

Phew! That was close!

"I'm sorry I thought you had gas issues," I say as I lean against the basement door. Acting like a barricade.

Hambone throws up his paws.

"What?" I say.

"What are you doing?" he says, looking completely baffled. "You need to open up that door and get out there."

"But there are zombie gorillas out there," I point out.

"Exactly," he says. "They need to see you, or my idea won't work."

"Oh, yeah, that's right," I say. "I'm sorry. Wasn't thinking. Won't happen again. Promise."

"Just get out there."

"Right," I say, hesitating. "Um, but before I do, can we just talk about your idea again?"

"What's there to talk about?" says Hambone. "It's all very simple. Zombie gorilla sees you. Likes you. Mmm, you nice lady. Me take you some place safe. Me take you to Evil Doctor Crazy Gorilla. I follow. We find the antidote. No more zombie gorillas. Human race safe. Incredibly famous. Yay!"

"OK, I get that," I say. "But I don't know. This is getting sooooo real all of a sudden."

"It wasn't before?" he says.

"Yeah, it was," I say. "But I don't know. Seeing the zombie gorillas, knowing they are just on the other side of this door—it's kind of a bit much. I don't think I can do this. I'm not up for it. I mean, what if he senses that I'm not a lady? Gorillas are pretty smart, you know. What if he says, 'You not lady. You kid in dress. Me not take you anywhere. Me eat your flesh off instead'?"

I start to lose it. Emotionally, I mean. Get a little hysterical.

I'm trembling.

I'm shuddering.

"I can't do this," I blather. "I can't do this. They have fangs. They have fangs. Big yellow fangs. Sharp. Pointy. And they rip. And they tear. Flesh. Right off your bones. Just ripping and tearing. Tearing and ripping. The agony. The pain. The misery. The woe. Oh, woe is me. Woe is me."

Hambone steps up and slaps me across the face. "Get it together, Peas."

I regain my composure.

"Thank you," I say. "I needed that. I really did. Wow. I lost my head for a second there."

"We'll find it again," says Hambone. "The whole world needs you. And your head."

I take a deep breath.

"I got it," I say. "I'm good. Good to go."

I open the basement door but then close it back up again real quick.

"So you really think this is going to work?" I say.

"Trust me."

Yeah, that's a good one. The same kid who said to it was safe to jump out of a tree with a sled. Go slaloming down the snow bank. Right into oncoming traffic. Yeah. That was safe.

Oh, shnippies. What have I gotten myself into?

"Do I have to count to three?" says Hambone.

"No," I say. "I'm going to do this."

"So do it already—while we're young."

OK. This really is it. No more wavering. No more dithering. Just be brave.

I summon the courage.

I open the basement door.

Click. Click. Click. Click.

"Oh, look at me," I say, using my best impersonation of a lady's voice. "I'm just a lady out walking by myself. That's right. Lady here. Not a kid in a dress and silver earrings and a silver necklace and high heels and lipstick. Nope. Not trying to fool anyone. Not a trick. Genuine article. One hundred percent lady."

"Wow," says Hambone, calling out from behind the basement door. "Very convincing. You're probably going to have to beat the zombie gorillas off with a stick."

Very funny. I'd like to see him do better.

Just then, a zombie gorilla knuckle-walks up to me.

"Hey, you're kind of cute," I say. (Don't ask me why. It just sounded like something I should say.)

The zombie gorilla stares at me.

I stare back.

Can you say awkward?

As it stares at me, the zombie gorilla lowers its eyebrows and curls its lips back, exposing every inch of his big, yellow fangs.

This isn't good. It's not buying it. Not for one second.

What was I thinking agreeing to this idea? Stupidest idea ever!

Drool pours out of the corners of the zombie gorilla's mouth. It reminds me of Carl Spagano. He's this kid at my school. A fifth grader. Big oaf. Drools all the time. I think his parents give him hormones. I think he chews them like vitamins. Should start calling him "zombie gorilla boy." Hey, that's kind of funny. I'll have to tell Hambone that one. If I make it out of this alive.

The zombie gorilla starts pounding its chest and whooping.

I brace myself.

Hambone's idea is about to work, or I'm about to die. I sure hope it's the first one.

The zombie gorilla lunges out and grabs me. Wraps me up in its arms. Tight.

Oh, my shneggies! This is crazy. This is crazy.

I'm feeling faint. The world around me gets darker. Like somebody turning the lights off one by one. Goodbye, cruel world. It's getting darker and darker. And then: all the lights go off.

Chapter Twelve

come to.

Wow.

So that's what fainting is like. Huh. Have to say, not a big fan. But I guess I shouldn't complain. It's better than what could have happened: that zombie gorilla eating all my flesh off.

Wait a second. Am I getting ahead of myself here? Is all my flesh eaten off?

I give myself a pat down, checking to make sure all my flesh is where it's supposed to be.

It is.

Phew.

OK.

Had to check. Can't go around fleshless, now can I? That would give a whole new meaning to the word *naked*.

I look around.

This place is...um...what's the word I'm looking for? Um? How about dirty? No. Creepy? No. Cavey? No. Gloomy? No. Spidery? No. Spider-cobwebery? Is that even a word? No. Dungeony? Closer. Maybe I need more than one word. Maybe the best way to describe this place is dirty-creepy-cavey-gloomy-spidery-cobwebery-dugeony-H-E-double-hockey-sticks.

That last part I just added for effect. But you get the point—it's not a pleasant place.

So I'm getting out of here.

I go over to the door. It's locked. So now I'm being treated like a common criminal? That's not very cool. Let's add a new descriptive word for this place: jaily.

Uh-oh.

I hear footsteps. Someone is coming.

Hide. Hide. I have to hide. But where? Unfortunately, there isn't anything in here but me.

What to do? What to do?

I stand really still. Maybe whoever is coming won't see me.

This is ridiculous. Who am I kidding? I'm wearing a dress, silver earrings, a silver necklace, high heels, and lipstick. Who isn't going to see that?

I decide to hide in the corner, curling up into a tight ball. Again, not the smartest move, but it's my best option under the circumstances.

A key turns in the lock.

The door opens.

It's Hambone.

"Hey," he says. "See? Didn't I tell you this was going to work? Talk about nailing it. Come on, get up. Give me a high five. I deserve a little congratulations here. What an idea." He pauses, lost in thought. "That could be the title of the book they write about us: *Hambone's Amazing, Incredible, Spectacularly Awesome Idea to Save the World from Flesh-Eating Zombie Gorillas.* Yeah. That about sums it up."

"Really?" I say, getting up off the floor. "That's what you're calling it? How about we call it *How Hambone Got His Best Friend to Dress Up Like a Lady and Get Carried Away by a Flesh-Eating Zombie Gorilla*? And let's not forget the sequel: *What Is This Place*?"

"Relax," says Hambone. "We're exactly where we want to be: Evil Doctor Crazy Gorilla's secret hideout."

"That's supposed to make me feel better?" I say.

"It should."

"Well, it doesn't," I say, straightening out my dress. "So where is this secret hideout, anyway?"

"Take a guess."

"Just tell me," I say. I'm not in the mood to guess.

"Come on," says Hambone. "What's the fun it that? Take a guess."

"No."

"Fine," Hambone sniffs. "Be a baby. Take all the fun out of me telling you we're underneath the Gorilla Kingdom."

"Underneath?"

"Yeah," says Hambone, suddenly brightening. "It was pretty cool. So we get to the Gorilla Kingdom, and I'm all like, oh, no, it's just taking you back to where it was born—because, right, technically, the Gorilla Kingdom is where the ordinary gorilla turned into the zombie gorilla, so that is like its birthplace. And I was kind of bummed because I was so sure my idea was going to work. But then the zombie gorilla jumps up on the fallen log and yanks on this tree branch sticking out. But it's not a tree branch—it's a lever that looks like a tree branch—and all of a sudden, this rock slides out of the way, and there's this tunnel, and the zombie gorilla just goes right in and climbs down, and here we are."

"Great," I say. "I'm glad it all worked out so well in the end."

"Come, on," says Hambone. "Don't be all Mr. Grumpypants." He stops. He thinks. Then he flashes me a mischievous smile. "Um, I mean, that is, don't be all Mrs. Grumpypants." He starts laughing. "Aw, who am I kidding? Who's going to marry you? You're one ugly lady." He breaks down laughing.

"Now is not the time for jokes," I say, a little annoyed.

"I know, I know," he says. "But seriously. This is precisely the place we wanted that zombie gorilla to take you."

"Yeah, but I could have been killed in the process. Or worse."

"Yeah, but you weren't," says Hambone matter-of-factly. "Besides, you were never in any real danger. I was following you the whole time. Never more than two steps behind. And I would have opened up a can of whup-butt on that zombie gorilla the second I thought it was going to take a bite."

I hate to admit it because I'm not totally over this whole spectacularly awesome idea of Hambone's just yet, but hearing him say he was right there does make me feel better. I tell him this.

"Good," he says. "Because what we have to do now is find the antidote. Right? So let's go do that."

"OK," I say. "But before we do do that—"

"That's a lot of dodo."

I give Hambone a look. "Very funny," I say. "Before we *do* that, tell me something: Where did you get the key?"

"You mean this one?" says Hambone, holding up the key for inspection. "I told you, I never let you out of my sight. So when Evil Doctor Crazy Gorilla locked you in here, I watched what he did with it after."

"Wait a second," I say, momentarily taken aback. "You saw Evil Doctor Crazy Gorilla?"

"Well, it is his secret hideout underneath the Gorilla Kingdom, isn't it? Or haven't you been listening?"

"But if you saw him, did you also see the antidote?"

"It's not like the key," he says. "He didn't have it on him."

"Wait a second," I say, even more taken aback. "You got the key off of Evil Doctor Crazy Gorilla?"

"How else was I going to get it?" says Hambone, giving me a look. "He put it back in his coat pocket."

I shake my head. "Don't look at me like I have brain damage. I fainted. So I have no idea about any of this. So it would be nice if you would just fill in the blanks for me, OK?"

"Fine," says Hambone. "I'll even go slow for you as well, OK? Evil Doctor Crazy Gorilla puts key back in pocket, goes with zombie gorilla back to his laboratory, does his mad-scientist stuff, falls asleep, I tiptoe over, take key out, come back here, open door, see you, say, 'Yeah!'"

"You've seen his laboratory?"

Hambone drops his head. "Boy, are you sure you didn't suffer any brain damage as a result of your fainting? Because I'm starting to feel like I'm talking to a moron here."

"Hey," I say. "That's not fair."

"What, to morons?" Hambone flashes me a mischievous grin.

"Whatever," I say, getting annoyed. "It's not my fault I fainted. I bet you would have done the exact same thing if you were in my place—oh wait, that's right, you weren't in my place. So walk a mile in my shoes before you make jokes. How about that?"

"I think your heels are too high for me," says Hambone, barely able to suppress another mischievous grin.

"Aaugh!" I scream. I'm so angry at him right now.

Hambone knows it too. Because he walks over to me, his tail between his legs.

"Bad dog," he says, playfully slapping his paw.

I ignore him. It's going to take more than that to get me to forgive him.

"I'm sorry," he continues. "Sometimes I just can't control myself. I say things that I think are funny. It's one of my many bad habits. But I am sorry. What you did was momentous. It was historic. Earth shattering. And you should be proud. I know I'm proud of you."

Boy, Hambone sure has outdone himself. I've never heard him apologize like that before. In fact, I've never heard him apologize, period. I guess you *can* teach an old dog new tricks.

"Do you forgive me?" he says.

I do.

"All right, then," he says, slapping his paws together. "Time is a wasting. Let's go get us some antidote." He turns and points at the door. "Follow me. This way to Evil Doctor Crazy Gorilla's laboratory."

Chapter Thirteen

Tunnels. Tunnels. And more tunnels.

"Are you sure you know where you're going, Hambone?" I say, stopping to catch my breath. "It feels like we've been going around in circles."

"I hate to admit it," says Hambone, "but I didn't really pay any attention when I followed Evil Doctor Crazy Gorilla and that zombie gorilla back to the laboratory. I figured I could always find them again with my nose if I had to."

"So what's the problem?"

Hambone sniffs the air. "Do you smell that?"

"You're asking me?" I say. "That's kind of funny, isn't it? You know your sense of smell is about a million times better than mine."

"No, I know. But do you smell that?"

I take a whiff. "I actually don't smell anything," I say. "Is that what happens when you faint—you lose your sense of smell?"

"Well, if you do, it's a good thing because that means you can't smell the stench of zombie gorilla," says Hambone. "That's what I smell. Pee-yew! Can't get it out of my nostrils. And it's not getting any stronger, which isn't good."

"Why not?" I say.

"Because that's how I know I'm getting closer—the scent gets stronger," says Hambone. "But this, this is like a constant stench—it doesn't get stronger or weaker—it just stays the same. I don't understand it."

"Maybe being underground does something to your sense of smell," I say.

"I don't know," says Hambone. He starts sniffing. "This is weird." He keeps sniffing. "It's like..." He comes right up to me, still sniffing. "Whoa," he says, putting his paws up. "There we go. Now I got it."

"Got what?"

"No wonder I'm thrown off here," he says, putting his nose to my dress and sniffing deeply. "You reek of zombie gorilla."

"I do?" Oh, great. You know how much I hate the smell of gorillas. Now I smell like a zombie gorilla? "How come I can't smell it, do you think?"

"It's probably like when you smell something for a long time, you can't smell it anymore," says Hambone. "It's like you've become immune to it or something."

"Great," I say. "I don't want to be immune to this. I want to get rid of it. How am I going to do that? Take a bath in tomato juice?"

"That's for skunk spray," says Hambone. "Maybe you should try gasoline."

"Maybe I should just scrape my skin off."

"Now, now," says Hambone, shaking his head. "You don't want to do that. But what you do want to do is stand about forty feet behind me." He shoos me away from him. "That's right. Keep going. The farther behind the better. That way I won't be smelling you the whole time. Perfect."

I'm standing about forty feet behind him.

"How you doing back there?" says Hambone, smiling reassuringly. "Now don't worry. I'll wait for you before I do anything."

He starts walking down the tunnel.

Before I know it, he's standing outside the door to Evil Doctor Crazy Gorilla's laboratory.

"What's the plan?" I say, catching up to him.

"What do you mean, what's the plan?" says Hambone, giving me a look. "The plan is we go in there and get the antidote."

"Just like that?" I say.

"Yeah," he says. "Just like that. We are on a mission here, you know. A mission to save the world. And we're so close I can taste it."

Hambone looks me in the eyes. "On the count of three: one—two—three!"

We burst into Evil Doctor Crazy Gorilla's laboratory. What the...?

Evil Doctor Crazy Gorilla is nowhere to be seen. The only thing to be seen is all his laboratory stuff. On a table are beakers and test tubes filled with all different colored liquids: red and green and yellow and pink and blue. There's smoke billowing out of them. Like lava. Wires and plugs and other contraptions hang from the ceiling. As if someone spent hours sticking them up there. On another table are dissecting tools: knives, scalpels, pliers, razor blades. A bottle with a stopper sits on the table as well. As does a big bowl.

There's more, but I don't have time to tell you about it. Because someone is coming.

Me and Hambone duck behind the door.

Just then, in walks Evil Doctor Crazy Gorilla and the zombie gorilla that took me. They go over to the table with the beakers and test tubes.

Hambone slams the door shut. The sound startles Evil Doctor Crazy Gorilla. He looks over at us. "What's going on here?" he says. He doesn't wait for us to answer. Instead, he looks directly at me. "How did you escape?"

"I let him out," says Hambone.

"You?" says Evil Doctor Crazy Gorilla. "Who are you?"

"I'm the kid who's going to open up a can of whup-butt on you if you don't hand over the antidote," says Hambone, smirking.

"You're a kid?" says Evil Doctor Crazy Gorilla, looking perplexed. "You look like a dog to me."

I jump in. "Well, he's not a dog, but a kid;, even though he doesn't look like a kid, he looks like a dog. But he shouldn't be a kid right now—he should be a dog." I go over to Hambone and slap him on the nose. "Bad dog. Bad, bad dog."

Hambone pushes me away. "Get out of here, stupid. It's not like it matters. Even if this guy told anybody about me, do you think they'd believe him? No. He's Evil Doctor Crazy Gorilla. Trying to take over the world with zombie gorillas. He's not a sane person."

Evil Doctor Crazy Gorilla looks at Hambone. "So if you're a dog that's a kid, what's he?" He points at me.

"What does it look like?" says Hambone. "He's a kid dressed like a lady."

"Is this a joke?" says Evil Doctor Crazy Gorilla, looking around. "Am I on one of those hidden-camera shows? Is somebody going to jump out any second and say, 'Smile!'?" He keeps looking around. "So where are the cameras?"

"There aren't any cameras, you crazy weirdo," says Hambone. "There's just us: Peas and Hambone. So you'd better hand over that antidote. I'm not going to ask you again."

Evil Doctor Crazy Gorilla picks up a test tube filled with red liquid. "You mean *this* antidote?" he says, holding the test tube out to us and then pulling it back right away. "Is *this* the one you mean? *This* one?" He holds it out to us again and then pulls it right back. Again.

He's mocking us. He thinks we're not serious. I'll show him serious.

"If you don't give it to us, we'll take it," I say.

Evil Doctor Crazy Gorilla laughs. "I'd like to see you try."

"Stand back," says Hambone. "I'll take it from here."

He takes a step forward.

GRRRR!

The zombie gorilla beats his chest and then starts knuckle-walking toward Hambone. Oh, no. It's going into protect mode. Which means stopping Hambone before he gets any closer.

Hambone pauses. I think he knows he's in trouble. He doesn't have a weapon. At least not one he can reach from where he's standing.

Luckily, Evil Doctor Crazy Gorilla puts out his arm and stops the zombie gorilla from going after Hambone. He whispers something in its ear. Probably more of that gorilla-whisperer stuff. The zombie gorilla turns and looks at Hambone. It hoots at him. Like it's telling Hambone that he's lucky it didn't have the chance to go at him. And he might not be so lucky the next time. Then it goes over into the corner and sits down.

I look over at Hambone. He smiles. "He just made it that much easier for me," he says, winking at me. "Ready or not, here I come."

He starts running for Evil Doctor Crazy Gorilla.

When Hambone gets within inches, Evil Doctor Crazy Gorilla presses a button on the table. A metal cage drops from the ceiling, landing directly on top of Hambone. He's trapped. "Let me out of here," he says, shaking the bars.

It's no use. He gives up.

"Well," he says, looking at me, "what are you waiting for? Go get him!"

I start. I stop. I hesitate. What else does Evil Doctor Crazy Gorilla have up his sleeve? I bet he's just waiting for me to take a run at him. Then he can unleash another one of his diabolical traps.

Turns out I don't have to take a run at him to find out.

Evil Doctor Crazy Gorilla pushes another button on the table. A column of smoke rises from the ground. It swirls around me, wrapping me in a cloudy straitjacket.

This can't be good.

I try not to breathe the smoke, but I can't help it. Some gets up into my nostrils, as if it's forcing its way in. Boy, whatever this stuff is, it's sinister. I mean, there's no stopping it. It's making me woozy.

Evil Doctor Crazy Gorilla comes over to me. He grabs my hand and leads me across the laboratory.

"Where are we going?" I think I say. I'm not sure. I can't see clearly. I can't even think clearly. I'm just woozy.

"Just relax, kid," I hear Evil Doctor Crazy Gorilla saying. Or did I?

The next thing I know, I'm being helped onto a cot pushed up against the wall. Evil Doctor Crazy Gorilla tucks my arms against my sides and turns my hands palm up. Then he spreads my legs apart so that my feet touch the corners of the cot.

"All of this will be over very soon," says Evil Doctor Crazy Gorilla.

This time I know I heard that. The cloud is suddenly lifting. I can see clearly again. And think clearly again.

"What's going on?" I say. "What was that stuff?"

"Just something I created," he says. "It momentarily incapacitates people. Makes it easier for me to get them to do whatever I want them to do. Especially if it's against their will."

Against their will? What does that mean?

Uh-oh. I know what that means.

I try to move my arms but can't—they're strapped against the cot. Same goes for my feet. And it feels like the more I struggle, the tighter the straps get.

I lift my head off the cot and look down at my arms and feet. I want to know what exactly Evil Doctor Crazy Gorilla has done to me.

"Now, now," says Evil Doctor Crazy Gorilla. "Don't worry your little head about it. Just leave it to me."

He steps behind me and straps my head down.

Just then I hear a whirling noise followed by a series of beeps. It kind of reminds me of the noises a computer makes when you first start it up. But I don't remember seeing any computers in the laboratory.

So where are the noises coming from?

Oh-my-shneggies!

Now I know. Lowering down from the ceiling is a wire with a syringe attached. The syringe stops inches from my face. I can see that it is filled with the same green potion Evil Doctor Crazy Gorilla gave the gorillas in the clearing.

More strange noises.

This time two small boxes open in the wall above me. Then a mechanical hand slides out from each box. They reach down and grab hold of my mouth, prying it open like a pistachio nut.

No! No! No! I get what's going on. Evil Doctor Crazy Gorilla is going to give me some of the green potion. Why? Does he want to turn me into a zombie gorilla? What if it doesn't work? Maybe it only turns gorillas into zombie gorillas. Maybe it turns kids into chicken boys. I don't want to be a chicken boy. I don't want to be a chicken boy at all. I don't want to live in a chicken coop. I don't want to lay eggs. What do I want? I want none of this to be happening to me.

"Thaawww! Leazzze! Thaawww!" I'm trying to say, "Stop! Please! Stop!" But under the circumstances it's the best I can do. But who am I kidding? He's not going to stop. He's going to inject that green potion into my mouth, and there's nothing I can do about it.

"Don't do it," says Hambone. "Don't even think about giving that potion garbage to my best friend."

"Don't you think he would like being a zombie?" says Evil Doctor Crazy Gorilla. "I thought all kids wanted to be zombies."

So it's going to turn me into a zombie? Greeeeeaaaaaat!

"Don't do it," repeats Hambone. "I'm warning you."

"Really?" says Evil Doctor Crazy Gorilla. "You're warning me? Says the little doggie—oh, wait. You're not a little doggie. You're a little kid who looks like a little doggie. That's right. My mistake. Let me try it again. Says the little kid who looks like a little doggie—in a cage."

"Not for long," says Hambone. "You'd better be afraid. Be very, very afraid. I'm almost out of here. And when I'm out, I have a can of whup-butt here with your name on it."

Evil Doctor Crazy Gorilla cackles. "You don't get it," he says. "It's over! I win! You lose! Ha! Ha! Ha! You think you can mess with me? I don't think so! I own you! And soon I'm going to own the world! It'll be mine! All mine! And there's nothing you or anybody else can do to stop me! I'm unstoppable! I'm the greatest! I'll soon be the ruler of the entire world!"

"Wow, somebody sure has an overinflated sense of himself," says Hambone. "But I guess if you're trying to eliminate the human race and replace it with zombie gorillas that you control, your elevator doesn't go all the way to the top, if you know what I'm saying. You're a few fries short of a Happy Meal. You're not the brightest crayon in the box. You're one spring short of a slinky. You're a few peas short of a casserole. No offense, Peas."

None taken.

"You think I'm crazy?" says Evil Doctor Crazy Gorilla. "I'd like you to know that I have one of the finest scientific minds of my generation. Crazy person. Would a crazy person come up with such an ingenious plan? I don't think so. I'd like to see somebody else take ordinary gorillas and turn them into an army of zombie gorillas dogged in their quest for human flesh. No pun intended. But enough talk. The time for talking is over."

What's he doing now? I try to look out of the corner of my eye to see what's happening.

"Hang in there, Peas," says Hambone. "If you can, try not to swallow."

Seriously? I don't think I'm going to have any choice.

Evil Doctor Crazy Gorilla comes up to the cot. He stands over me. "I don't really know if you are going to turn into a zombie. I've never tested this on human beings before, but what the heck. Whatever happens, happens, right?"

I try to speak again.

"What was that?" says Evil Doctor Crazy Gorilla, putting his hand to his ear. "Did you say something?" He presses a button, and the two hands let go of my mouth. "Speak now, or forever hold your peace."

"Hey, wait a second," I say. "You say you have a great scientific mind? Then you'd know that it isn't ethical to conduct a blind experiment on a human being. It's against the oath all scientists have to take. I know. I'm going to be a scientist someday. But you obviously don't know. So you must not be a real scientist. You're just a fake."

I'm just making this stuff up, totally winging it, but I figure it's worth a shot. What have I got to lose?

"How do you know about the oath?" says Evil Doctor Crazy Gorilla.

"There is such a thing?" I say.

"No," he says. "Now say ah."

Evil Doctor Crazy Gorilla reaches up for the syringe. I close my eyes.

What a way to go. If I could shake my head in disbelief, I would.

Just then, I see something moving toward me out of the corner of my eye. It's Hambone. Somehow he got out. And now he's sneaking up behind Evil Doctor Crazy Gorilla.

WHUMP!

Hambone wallops Evil Doctor Crazy Gorilla right in the back of the head, knocking him out cold.

"How does that can of whup-butt taste?" says Hambone, raising his arms in victory.

GRRRR!

Uh-oh.

Can you say angry zombie gorilla? Judging by the look on its face, it didn't care too much for that can of whup-butt Hambone opened up on Evil Doctor Crazy Gorilla. In fact, I think it is going to take that can of whup-butt and shove it down Hambone's throat.

Poor Hambone. What a short-lived victory.

Hambone looks around for a weapon. Nothing is close by.

"Quick," I say. "Press the button on the table. It's your only option."

Hambone presses the button. Smoke rises up and covers the zombie gorilla. It stops moving forward. It just stays where it is, rocking slightly from side to side.

"Now what?" says Hambone.

"Get me out of here," I say. He does.

I go over and pick up the test tube filled with red liquid. I figure why not give the zombie gorilla some of the antidote? So I do. It's amazing. In like seconds it changes back into an ordinary gorilla.

"Now let's put him in the cage," I say.

"OK," says Hambone. "But first we have to fill up the hole that I dug to escape."

"So that's how you did it," I say, helping him put the dirt back in the hole. "I was about to ask you."

"Well, I am kind of an expert at digging holes," says Hambone, stamping down on the dirt to pack it tighter. "But if you want to know the truth, I kind of owe it all to you."

"To me?" I say, taken aback.

"Yeah," he says. "If it weren't for you going on and on and on with that scientist gibberish, I never would have gotten out in time. That bought me the precious extra seconds I needed."

"Glad my desperate bid to save myself from being turned into a...I don't know. Probably a cross between a kid dressed like a lady, a chicken boy, and a zombie gorilla—whatever that is—glad you could use that to your advantage." Since you can't tell, my tongue is firmly in my cheek when I say that.

Hambone doesn't have a clue. It goes right over his head.

"OW! Ow, ow, ow."

Speaking of heads, Evil Doctor Crazy Gorilla is rubbing the back of his head and attempting to get to his feet. We help him do that. In fact, we help him right off his feet and onto the cot. "There, there," I say. "Don't you worry your little head about it. Just leave it to me."

I strap him down just the way he did to me.

I look at Hambone. He looks at me.

"How do you like us now?" he says.

We give each other jumping high fives.

We did it.

We stopped Evil Doctor Crazy Gorilla.

We saved the world.

It's good to be Peas and Hambone.

Epilogue

We handed the antidote over to the proper authorities. They thanked us. They thanked us a lot. In fact, they thanked us so much they said the only proper way to thank us was to give us a reward. After all, we did save the human race.

Hambone kept elbowing me in the side as we waited to hear what our reward was, whispering to me to hold my breath because it was going to be huge.

I told him to stop whispering. I didn't want any of the proper authorities to know that he's not a dog but a kid even though he doesn't look like a kid, he looks like a dog. It probably would not have gone over so well.

But Hambone kept at it. He kept whispering that I should hold my breath.

Don't hold your breath. It wasn't huge. Just the opposite.

How unhuge? Well, it wasn't statues made in our likeness. Not diamonds. Not Lamborghinis. Not even cold, hard cash. None of that.

Are you ready for what they did give us?

Here goes: a lifetime membership to the zoo.

Swear. That's what they gave us.

I didn't think it was that bad.

Hambone, of course, was so upset he nearly had a seizure.

You ever try to give CPR to a dog? Me neither.

I had to think of something to calm him down. So I reminded him that we like going to the zoo. We used to do it all the time before you-know-what happened. (Think the one about the curious incident with the gorilla and a handful of dirt.) And so, since we now have this membership, we should at least go back and make nicey-nice with the gorillas. On account of I don't think we'll ever find out which gorilla was the one that threw the dirt in the first place, I figured it was best to be nice to all of them.

Hambone agreed—reluctantly. And I mean very reluctantly. I had to drag him kicking and barking all the way there. Talk about a doggy fit.

Once we got to the zoo, it wasn't much better. He was still kicking and barking. So I had to tell him if he didn't stop, I was going to start coming to the zoo without him. Leave him at home chained up in the backyard.

That did it.

And I have to say he did a nice job of being nice. He called out to each and every gorilla in the clearing and said he was sorry, that he wanted to have a truce, that burying the hatchet was the thing to do. He said that from now on, we should enjoy one another's company.

It was priceless. I wish I had a video camera so I could put it up on YouTube. We may not have become famous for saving the world from Evil Doctor Crazy Gorilla and his army of zombie gorillas, but once that video went viral, the fame would have come to us.

Oh, well.

We stood and chitchatted awhile longer, but then it was time to go. We said our good-byes and started to leave.

I was proud of Hambone. And I was about to tell him this when all of a sudden, a handful of dirt smacked him right in the back of the head—thwap!

The gorilla responsible started jumping up and down, laughing hysterically.

I looked at Hambone.

Boy, was he mad.

Don't do it, I told him. Don't do what I know you're going to do. Be better than that. Be a bigger dog.

But do you think he listened to me?

Of course not.

But that's a story for another time.

Made in the USA
Lexington, KY
21 January 2014